THE BEST *of*

BETTY NEELS

HILLTOP TRYST

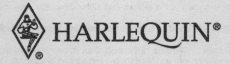

HARLEQUIN®

TORONTO • NEW YORK • LONDON
AMSTERDAM • PARIS • SYDNEY • HAMBURG
STOCKHOLM • ATHENS • TOKYO • MILAN • MADRID
PRAGUE • WARSAW • BUDAPEST • AUCKLAND

ISBN 0-373-51131-0

HILLTOP TRYST

First North American Publication 2001

Visit us at www.eHarlequin.com

Printed in U.S.A.

Dear Reader,

Looking back over the years, I find it hard to realize that twenty-six of them have gone by since I wrote my first book—*Sister Peters in Amsterdam*. It wasn't until I started writing about her that I found that once I had started writing, nothing was going to make me stop—and at that time I had no intention of sending the manuscript to a publisher. It was my daughter who urged me to try my luck.

I shall never forget the thrill of having my first book accepted. And it's still a thrill each time a new story is accepted. Writing is such a pleasure to me, and seeing a story unfolding on my old typewriter is like watching a film and wondering how it will end. Happily, of course.

To have so many of my books republished is such a delightful thing to happen, and I can only hope that those who read them will share my pleasure in seeing them on the bookshelves again...and will enjoy reading them.

Betty Neels

Betty Neels spent her childhood and youth in Devonshire before training as a nurse and midwife. She was an army nursing sister during the war, married a Dutchman and subsequently lived in Holland for fourteen years. She now lives with her husband in Dorset and has a daughter and grandson. Her hobbies are reading, animals, old buildings and, of course, writing. Betty started to write upon retirement from nursing, incited by a lady in a library bemoaning the lack of romantic novels. She has since become one of Harlequin's most prolific and well-loved authors.

CHAPTER ONE

THE SUN, rising gloriously on the morning of Midsummer's Day, turned the swelling Dorset hills into a wide vista of golden green fields and clumps of trees under a blue sky. Miles away, traffic along the dual carriageway thundered on its way to the west, unheard and unheeded in the quiet countryside around the village of Hindley, its inhabitants for the most part still sleeping in their beds. Farm workers were already about their work, though; the bleating of sheep and the sounds of horses and cattle were blotted out from time to time by the sound of a tractor being started up; but on the brow of the hill rising behind the village these sounds were faint, the birdsong was louder.

Half-way up the hill a girl sat, leaning comfortably against the trunk of a fallen tree, a shaggy dog sprawled beside her. She had drawn up her knees, clasped her arms around them and rested her chin on them—a pretty, rounded chin, but determined too, belying the wide, gentle mouth and the soft brown eyes with their thick black lashes. Her hair was long and brown, plaited and hanging over one shoulder. She flung it back with a well-shaped hand and spoke to the dog.

'There—the sun's rising on the longest day of the year, Knotty. Midsummer Madness—the high tide of the year, a day for fairies and elves, a day for making a wish. Do you suppose if I made one it might come true?'

Knotty, usually obliging with his replies, took no notice, but growled softly, cocked his large, drooping ears and allowed his teeth to show. He got to his feet and she put a restraining hand on his collar, turning to look behind her as she caught the sound of steady feet and someone coming along, whistling.

Knotty barked as a man left the line of trees and came towards them. A giant of a man, dressed in an open-necked shirt and elderly trousers, his pale hair shone in the sunlight and he walked with an easy self-assurance. Tucked under one arm was a small dog, a Jack Russell, looking bedraggled.

He stopped by the girl, towering over her so that she was forced to crane her neck to see his face. 'Good morning. Perhaps you can help me?' He had put down a balled fist for Knotty to examine, ignoring the teeth.

'I found this little chap down a rabbit-hole—couldn't get out and probably been there for some time. Is there a vet around here?' He smiled at her. 'The name's Latimer—Oliver Latimer.'

The girl got to her feet, glad for once that she was a tall girl, and very nearly able to look him in the face. 'Beatrice Browning. That's Nobby—Miss Mead's dog. She'll be so very glad, he's been missing for a couple of days—everyone has been out looking for him. Where was he?'

'About a mile on the other side of these woods—there's a stretch of common land... The vet?'

'You'd better come with me. Father will be up by now; he's leaving early to visit a couple of farms.'

She started down the hill towards the village below. 'You're out early,' she observed.

'Yes. You too. It's the best time of the day, isn't it?'

She nodded. They had left the hill behind them and were in a narrow rutted lane, the roofs of the village very close.

'You live here?' he wanted to know. He spoke so casually that she decided that he was merely making polite conversation.

'My home is here; I live with an aunt in Wilton.' She turned to look at him. 'Well, not all the time—I'm staying with her until she can get another companion.' She went on walking. 'Actually she's a great-aunt.'

She frowned; here she was, handing out information which couldn't be of the slightest interest to this man. She said austerely, 'What a splendid day it is. Here we are.' Her father's house was of a comfortable size surrounded by a large, overgrown garden, and with a paddock alongside for any animals he might need to take under his care. She led the way around the side of the house, so in through the back door, and found her father sitting on the doorstep drinking tea. He wished her good morning and looked enquiringly at her companion. 'A patient already—bless me, that's Nobby! Hurt?'

'Nothing broken, I fancy. Hungry and dehydrated, I should imagine.'

'Mr Latimer found him down a rabbit-hole the other side of Billings Wood,' said Beatrice. 'My father,' she added rather unnecessarily.

The two men shook hands, and Nobby was handed over to be examined by her father. Presently he said, 'He seems to have got off very lightly. There's no reason why he shouldn't go straight back to Miss Mead.'

'If you will tell me where to go, I'll take him as I walk back.'

Beatrice had poured the tea into two mugs. 'Have some tea first,' she offered. 'Do you want to phone anyone? This must have delayed you...'

'Stay for breakfast?' suggested her father. 'My wife will be down directly—I want to be well away before eight o'clock.' He glanced up. 'Far to go?'

'Telfont Evias—I'm staying with the Elliotts.'

'George Elliott? My dear chap, give him a ring and say you're staying for breakfast. It's all of three miles. Beatrice, will you show him where the telephone is? You can take Nobby back while breakfast is being cooked.'

Miss Mead lived right in the village in one of the charming cottages which stood on either side of the main street. Trees edged the cobbled pavement and the small front gardens were a blaze of colour. Mr Latimer strolled along beside Beatrice, Nobby tucked under one arm, talking of this and that in his deep voice. Quite nice, but a bit placid, Beatrice decided silently, peeping sideways at his profile. He was undoubtedly good-looking as well as being extremely large. Much, much larger than James, the eldest son of Dr Forbes, who had for some time now taken it for granted that she would marry him when he asked her...

She decided not to think about him for the moment, and instead pointed out the ancient and famous inn on the corner of the street and suggested that they might cross over, since Miss Mead's little cottage was on the other side.

Miss Mead answered their knock on her door. She was tall and thin and elderly, and very ladylike. She wore well-made skirts and blouses, and covered them with cardigans of a suitable weight according to the time of year, and drove a small car. She was liked in the village, but guardedly so, for she had an acid tongue if annoyed.

But now her stern face crumpled into tearful delight. 'Nobby—where have you been?' She took him from Mr Latimer and hugged him close.

'You found him. Oh, I'm so grateful, I can never thank you enough—I've hardly slept...'

She looked at them in turn. 'He's not hurt? Has your father seen him, Beatrice?'

'Yes, Miss Mead. Mr Latimer found him down a rabbit-hole and carried him here.'

'He seems to have come to no harm,' interpolated Mr Latimer in his calm voice. 'Tired and hungry and thirsty—a couple of days and he'll be quite fit again.'

'You're so kind—really, I don't know how to thank you…'

'No need, Miss Mead. He's a nice little chap.' He turned to Beatrice. 'Should we be getting back? I don't want to keep your father waiting.'

A bit cool, she thought, agreeing politely, wishing Miss Mead goodbye and waiting while she shook hands with her companion and thanked him once again. Perhaps his placid manner hid arrogance. Not that it mattered, she reflected, walking back with him and responding politely to his gentle flow of talk; they were most unlikely to meet again. A friend of the Elliotts, staying for a day or two, she supposed.

He proved to be a delightful guest. Her mother sat him down beside her and plied him with breakfast and a steady flow of nicely veiled questions, which he answered without telling her anything at all about himself. That he knew the Elliotts was a fact, but where he came from and what he did somehow remained obscure. All the same, Mrs Browning liked him, and Beatrice's three sisters liked him too, taking it in turns to engage him in conversation. And he was charming to them; Ella, fifteen and still at school, Carol, on holiday from the stockbroker's office where she worked in Salisbury, and Kathy, getting married in a few weeks' time...

They were all so pretty, thought Beatrice without rancour; she was pretty herself, but at twenty-six and as the eldest she tended to regard them as very much younger than herself, partly because they were all cast in a smaller mould and could get into each other's size tens, while she was forced to clothe her splendid proportions in a size fourteen.

Mr Latimer didn't overstay his welcome; when her father got up from the table he got up too, saying that he must be on his way. He thanked Mrs Browning for his breakfast, bade her daughters goodbye and left the house with Mr Browning, bidding him goodbye too as they reached the Land Rover parked by the gate and setting off at a leisurely pace in the direction of Telfont Evias.

'What a very nice man,' observed Mrs Browning, peering at his retreating back from the kitchen window. 'I do wonder...' She sighed silently and glanced at Beatrice, busy clearing the breakfast-table. 'I don't suppose we shall see him again—I mean, Lorna Elliott has never mentioned him.'

'Perhaps he's not a close friend.' Ella, on her way to get the school bus, kissed her mother and ran down the drive.

And after that no one had much more to say about him; there was the washing-up to do, beds to make, rooms to Hoover and dust and lunch to plan, and as well as that there were the dogs and cats to feed and the old pony in the paddock to groom.

Mr Browning came back during the morning, saw several patients, just had his coffee and then dashed away again to see a sick cow; and at lunch the talk was largely about Great-Aunt Sybil who lived in Wilton and to whom Beatrice was acting as a companion until some luckless woman would be fool enough to answer her advertisement. Beatrice had been there three weeks already, and that, she pointed out with some heat, was three weeks too long. She was only at home now because the old lady had taken herself off to London to be given her yearly check-up by the particular doctor she favoured. She was due back the next day, and Beatrice had been told to present herself at her aunt's house in the early afternoon.

'If it wasn't for the fact that she's family, I wouldn't go,' declared Beatrice.

'It can't be for much longer, dear,' soothed her mother, 'and I know it's asking a lot of you, but who else is there? Ella's too young, Carol's due back in two days' time and Kathy has such a lot to do before the wedding.'

Beatrice cast her fine eyes to the ceiling. 'If the worst comes to the worst, and no one applies for the job, I'd better get married myself.'

There was an instant chorus of, 'Oh, has James proposed?'

And Kathy added, 'I mean properly, and not just taking you for granted.'

'He's not said a word,' said Beatrice cheerfully, 'and even if he did I wouldn't...' She paused, quite surprised that she had meant exactly that.

Until that very moment she hadn't bothered too much about James, while at the back of her mind was the knowledge that when he felt like it he would ask her to marry him, or at least allow his intentions to show, but now she was quite sure that she wouldn't marry him if he were the last man on earth.

'Oh, good,' said Kathy. 'He's not at all your sort, you know.'

'No. I wonder why I didn't see that?'

'Well, dear—he may never ask you,' observed her mother.

'That's just what I mean,' went on Kathy, 'you would have dwindled into a long engagement while he deliberated about the future, and then got married without a scrap of romance.'

'Great-Aunt Sybil offers an alternative, doesn't she?' Beatrice laughed. 'I only hope she liked this doctor she went to see. And wouldn't it be wonderful if there were dozens of replies to her advert for a companion? Then I can come back home and help Father.'

Her father drove her over to Wilton the next day after an early lunch. 'I'm sorry about this, love,' he said as they drove the few miles to the town, 'but

your great-aunt is my mother's sister, and I did promise that I'd keep an eye on her.'

'And quite right too,' said Beatrice stoutly. 'Families should stick together.'

Her aunt's house was Georgian, its front door
opening on to the street which divided a square, tree-
lined and ringed around by similar roomy old houses.
Beatrice kissed her father goodbye, picked up her
case and pulled the bell by the door. Mrs Shadwell,
the sour-faced housekeeper, answered it and stood
aside so that she might go in, and with a final wave
to her father Beatrice went into the dim and gloomy
hall.

Her aunt hadn't returned yet; she went to her room
and unpacked her few things, and went downstairs
again to open the windows and the glass doors on to
the garden at the back of the house; her aunt would
order them all closed again the moment she came
into the house, but for the moment the warm sun lit
the heavily furnished room. Too nice to stay indoors,
decided Beatrice, and skipped outside. The garden
was quite large and mostly lawn bordered by shrubs
and a few trees. She went and sat down with her
back to one of them and allowed her thoughts to turn
to Mr Latimer. A nice man, she decided; a thought
dreamy, perhaps, and probably he had a bad temper
once roused. She wondered what he did for a living—a bank manager? A solicitor? Something to do
with television? Her idle thoughts were interrupted

by a sudden surge of movement within the house. Her aunt had returned.

Beatrice stayed where she was; she could hear her aunt's voice raised in umbrage and she sighed. It wouldn't have been so bad if she were paid for her companionship—if one could call it that: finding things, running up and down stairs with knitting, books, a scarf, answering the telephone, reading aloud to her aunt until that lady dozed off, only to wake a few minutes later and demand that she should continue reading and why had she stopped? Companion, Beatrice decided after a few days of this, wasn't the right word—there was no time to be a companion—who should have been someone to chat to and share jokes with and take little jaunts with on fine days. The word was slave.

Her aunt's voice, demanding to know where Miss Beatrice was, got her slowly to her feet and into the drawing-room.

'I'm here, Aunt.' She had a nice, quiet voice and a pleasant, calm manner. 'Did you have a good trip?'

'No, I did not. It was a waste of my time and my money—that old fool who saw me told me that I was as sound as a bell.'

She glared at Beatrice, who took no notice, but merely asked, 'But why don't you believe him, Aunt?'

'Because I know better; I am in constant pain, but I'm not one to moan and groan; I suffer in silence. You cannot possibly understand, a great healthy girl like you. I suppose you've been at home, idling away the days.'

'That's right, Aunt,' said Beatrice cheerfully. 'Nothing to do but help Father in the surgery, feed the animals, groom the pony and do some of the housework and the cooking...'

'Don't be impertinent, Beatrice! You may go upstairs to my room and make sure that Alice is unpacking my case correctly, and when you come down I wish you to get the telephone number of a heart specialist— No, on second thoughts you had better open the letters. There are bound to be answers to my advertisement.'

But from the little pile of letters Beatrice opened there were only three, and they didn't sound at all hopeful. The first one made it a condition that she should bring her cat with her, the second stipulated that she should have every other weekend free and the third expected the use of a car.

Beatrice offered them to her aunt without comment, and after they had been read and consigned to the wastepaper basket she observed, 'Perhaps if you offered a larger salary...?'

Her aunt's majestic bosom swelled alarmingly. 'The salary I offer is ample. What does my companion need other than a comfortable home and good food?'

'Clothes,' suggested Beatrice, 'make-up and so on, money for presents, probably they have a mother or father they have to help out, holidays...'

'Rubbish. Be good enough to take these letters to the post.'

A respite, even though brief; Beatrice lingered in the little town for as long as she dared, and when she got back she was rebuked for loitering. 'And I have made an appointment with this heart specialist. I shall see him on Wednesday next and you will accompany me. He has rooms in Harley Street.' She added in her loud, commanding voice, 'Jenkins will drive us, and I intend to visit several of these agencies in the hope that I may find someone suitable to be my companion.'

'What a good idea. There's bound to be someone on their books. Will you interview them here or there, Aunt?'

'You may safely leave such decisions to me.' Great-Aunt Sybil turned a quelling eye upon her, only Beatrice took no notice of it; she was a sensible girl as well as a pretty one and had quickly learnt to ignore her aunt's worse moments. There were plenty of Great-Aunt Sybils in the world and, tiresome though they were, they had families who felt it their duty to keep an eye on them. Only she hoped it wouldn't be too long before she could go back home again, which thought led to her wondering how Miss Mead's Nobby was doing and that led naturally to Mr Latimer. An interesting man, she reflected, if only because of his great size and good looks; she speculated as to his age and quickly married him off to a willowy blonde, small and dainty with everybody doing everything they could for her because of her clinging nature. There would be children too, a little girl and an older boy—two perhaps... She was forced to return to her prosaic world then, because her aunt wished for a glass of sherry. 'And surely you can do that for me,' she grumbled in her over-powering voice, 'although you don't look capable of anything, sitting there daydreaming.'

Beatrice poured the sherry, handed it to her aunt, then gave herself one, tossed it off and, feeling reck-less, poured a second one. Great-Aunt Sybil vibrated with indignation. 'Well, really, upon my word, Be-atrice, what would your father say if he could see you now? Worse, what would that young man of yours think or say?'

'James? He's not my young man, Aunt Sybil, and I have no intention of marrying him, and I expect that Father would offer me a third glass,' she answered politely and in a reasonable voice, which gave her aunt no opportunity to accuse her of im-pertinence...

That lady gave her a fulminating look; a paid com-panion would have been dismissed on the spot, but Beatrice was family and had every right to return home. She said in a conciliatory voice, 'I dare say that you have had several opportunities to marry. You were a very pretty young girl and are still a pretty woman.'

'Twenty-six on my last birthday, Aunt.'

Beatrice spoke lightly, but just lately faint doubts

about her future were getting harder to ignore. Somehow the years were slipping by; until her sudden certainty that she couldn't possibly marry James, she supposed that she had rather taken it for granted that she and James would marry, but now she knew that that wouldn't do at all. She didn't love him and she didn't think he loved her. Perhaps she was never to meet a man who would love her and whom she could love. It was getting a bit late in the day, she thought wryly.

'Time you were married and bringing up a family,' declared Aunt Sybil tartly. 'A woman's work...'

And one which her aunt had never had to do, reflected Beatrice. Perhaps if she had had a husband and a handful of children, she might not have become such a trying old lady: always right, always advising people how to do things she knew nothing about, always criticising and correcting, expecting everyone to do what she wanted at a moment's notice...

'Well,' said Beatrice naughtily, 'when you find another companion and I can go home again, perhaps I'll start looking for a husband.'

'Do not be impertinent, Beatrice,' was all her aunt said quellingly...

Wednesday came to break the monotony of the days, and since it was a lovely summer morning Beatrice got into a rather nice silky two-piece in a pale pearly pink, brushed her hair into a shining chignon, thrust

her feet into high-heeled sandals and got into the
elderly Daimler beside her aunt.

Her aunt eyed her with disapproval. 'Really, my
dear, you are dressed more in the manner of someone
going to a garden party than a companion.'

'But I'm not a companion,' observed Beatrice
sweetly. 'I'm staying with you because you asked me
to. And it's a lovely day,' she added, to clinch the
matter.

'We will lunch,' stated Great-Aunt Sybil in a cross
voice, 'and visit some of these agencies. The sooner
I can approve of a companion the better. You are
becoming frivolous, Beatrice.'

Beatrice said meekly, 'Yes, Aunt Sybil, perhaps
I'm having a last fling before I dwindle into being
an old maid.'

Jenkins drove them sedately Londonwards, and at
exactly the right time deposited them outside a narrow Regency house in a row of similar narrow
houses. Beatrice rang the bell and then followed her
aunt's majestic progress into a pleasant waiting-
room, where they were greeted by an elderly receptionist and asked to sit down.

'My appointment is for half-past eleven,' pointed
out Aunt Sybil, 'and it is exactly that hour.' She drew
an indignant breath so that her corsets creaked.

'That's right, Miss Browning.' The receptionist
spoke smoothly. 'But the doctor is engaged for the
moment.'

'I do not expect to be kept waiting.'

The receptionist smiled politely, picked up the telephone and became immersed in conversation. She was putting it down again when a door at the end of the room opened and a woman came out. Beatrice could hear her saying goodbye to someone on the other side of the door and sighed thankfully; any minute now and her aunt would be whisked away by the nurse who had come into the room.

'You will accompany me,' decreed her aunt. 'I may need your support.' She sailed in the wake of the nurse and was ushered through the door, and Beatrice, walking reluctantly behind her, came to a sudden halt. The eminent doctor, a cardiologist of the first rank, according to her aunt, coming forward to shake her aunt's hand, was Mr Latimer.

A rather different Mr Latimer, though; this elegant man in his sober grey suit and spotless linen was a far cry from the casual walker in his old trousers and shirt. He showed no surprise at the sight of her, but greeted her aunt quietly and then waited with a slightly lifted eyebrow until Great-Aunt Sybil said testily, 'Oh, this is a great-niece of mine. I have a delicate constitution and may require her support.'

Mr Latimer said 'How do you do?' to Beatrice with a blandness which led her to suppose that he had forgotten her completely, observed that he had an excellent nurse in attendance and asked in what way could he advise his patient?

'You are a very young man,' observed Miss

Browning in a suspicious voice. 'I trust that you are adequately trained to diagnose illness?'

Beatrice blushed and looked at her feet; her aunt was going to be awful.

'If I might know the nature of your illness?' asked Mr Latimer with just the right amount of professional dignity. He glanced at the folder on his desk, containing letters from various colleagues on the subject of Miss Browning.

Miss Browning fixed him with a cold stare. 'I suffer great pain in my chest. It is at times unendurable, but I do not wish to bother those around me with complaints: I have learnt to conceal my suffering. I think I may say that I have more than my share of courage and patience. The pain is here,' she patted her massive bosom gently, 'and I will explain exactly...'

Which she did at great length, while Dr Latimer sat quietly watching her, though now and again he took a quick look at Beatrice, still examining her feet and wishing the ground would open beneath her.

Presently he interrupted her aunt's flow of talk. 'Yes. Well, Miss Browning, I think the best thing is for me to examine you. If you will go with Nurse, she will prepare you.'

Miss Browning swept out, pausing by Beatrice to beg her in ringing tones to come to her aid of she were to fall faint. 'For this will be an ordeal.'

Beatrice mumbled and peeped across the room to where Dr Latimer sat behind his desk. He was looking at her and smiling, and after a moment she smiled back.

'Don't you miss your green fields and hills?' he asked.

She nodded. After a moment she said, 'I didn't expect to see you again.'

'No? I rather feel it was inevitable that somehow we should meet.'

He got up in response to the buzzer on his desk and went to the examination-room, leaving her to wonder what on earth he meant.

She had plenty of time to ponder his words, for it was quite fifteen minutes before he came back, and there was nothing in his face to tell her what his examination had revealed. He sat down and began to write until after another five minutes his patient came back.

Miss Browning swept in on a tide of ill temper, sat herself down and addressed herself in quelling tones to the impassive man sitting behind his desk.

'I very much doubt,' began Great-Aunt Sybil, 'if you are qualified to diagnose my particular illness. It seems to me that you have failed to appreciate my suffering.'

Dr Latimer appeared unworried. He said smoothly, 'Miss Browning, you have a sound heart; your pain is caused by indigestion. I will give you a diet which, if you choose to follow it, will dispel the pain. From what you have told me, your diet is too rich. I will write to your doctor and inform him of my diagnosis.'

He stood up and went to her chair. 'What a relief it must be to you that you are so splendidly healthy.' He offered a hand, and she had perforce to take it. 'Nurse will give you the diet sheet.'

He accompanied her to the door, and Beatrice was relieved to see that for once her aunt had met her match: Dr Latimer's silky manners screened a steely intention to be in command of the situation. They were ushered out without Miss Browning having the time to utter any of the telling replies she might have had in mind.

The nurse had gone ahead to open the waiting-room door, and for a moment Beatrice and Dr Latimer were alone.

He held out a large, firm hand. 'Goodbye for the present,' he said.

'Oh, do you intend to see my aunt again?'

'Er—no—but we shall meet again.' He gave her a charming smile. 'You don't live with your aunt?'

'Heavens, no! Her companion left and I'm staying with her until we can find another one.' She paused. 'I did tell you.'

Aunt Sybil had turned at the doorway and was looking back at them. 'Come at once, Beatrice. I am exhausted.'

'Dear, oh, dear,' murmured Dr Latimer at his most soothing, 'we must see about that companion, mustn't we?'

She thought that he was merely being comforting, but then, she didn't know him well.

Lunch was a stormy meal, taken at her aunt's favourite restaurant. Naturally it consisted of all the things Miss Browning had been advised not to eat, and while they ate she gave her opinion of doctors in general and Dr Latimer in particular. 'He should be struck off,' she declared.

'Whatever for?' asked Beatrice. 'I thought he had beautiful manners.'

'Pooh—any silly woman could have her head turned by the professional civility these men employ—I am able to see through such tricks.'

Beatrice poured the coffee. 'Aunt Sybil, I think you might at least give his advice an airing...'

'I shall do just as I see fit. We will go now to that agency I have written to; there must be any number of women needing work. Just look at the unemployment...'

But there was no one suitable, nor was there at the other two agencies they visited. Beatrice, a cheerful girl by nature, allowed herself to get despondent at the prospect of weeks of Great-Aunt Sybil's irascible company.

Only it wasn't to be weeks, after all. Three days after her aunt's visit to Dr Latimer, a letter came. The writer, having seen Miss Browning's advertisement, begged to apply for the post of companion, and was willing to present herself at an interview whenever it was convenient.

'Let her come this afternoon,' said Great-Aunt Sybil grandly. 'She sounds a sensible woman.'

'Well, she could hardly get here and back again today,' Beatrice pointed out. 'It's a London address—besides, there's the fare, she might not have it.'

'I cannot think what these people do with their money.'

'They don't have any—or not much to do anything with.'

Her aunt frowned. 'You have this habit of answering back, Beatrice—most unbecoming. Write a letter and tell her to come the day after tomorrow in the early afternoon. You had better take some money from my desk and enclose it.'

Beatrice, addressing the envelope to Miss Jane Moore, hoped fervently that she would be suitable.

It was obvious from the moment that she faced Great-Aunt Sybil in the drawing-room that she was not only suitable but quite capable of holding her own with the old lady. Polite but firm, she allowed Miss Browning to see that she had no intention of being a doormat—indeed, she stipulated that she should have regular hours of freedom and a day off each week—but she sweetened this by pointing out that she was able to undertake all secretarial duties, keep accounts, drive the car, and read aloud. 'I also have some nursing skills,' she added composedly.

Beatrice thought she looked exactly the right person to live with her aunt. Middle-aged, small and wiry, with her pepper and salt hair and a severe bun, Miss Moore exuded competence, good nature and firmness.

Whether she would be able to stand up to her great-aunt's peevish ill humours was another matter. At the moment, at any rate, her aunt seemed more than satisfied. Miss Moore was engaged with the option of a month's notice on either side, and agreed to come in two days' time, Miss Browning's good humour lasting long enough for her to arrange for Miss Moore to be collected with her luggage at the station.

'So now you can go home,' said Miss Browning ungratefully as she and Beatrice sat at dinner that evening. If Beatrice expected thanks, she got none, but that didn't worry her; she telephoned her mother, packed her bag, and at the end of the next day returned home.

It was lovely to be back in her own room again, to unpack and then go down to the kitchen and help her mother get the supper.

'Do you think she'll last, this Miss Moore?' asked her mother.

'I think she might. I mean, Great-Aunt Sybil's other companions have always been so timid, but not Miss Moore—one could think of her as a ward sister used to geriatrics—you know—quite unflustered, but very firm and kind.'

She paused in the enjoyable task of hulling straw-

berries. 'I shall get up early tomorrow and take
Knotty for a long walk before breakfast.'

'Yes, dear. Your father will be glad to have you
back to give a hand. Carol's back in Salisbury and
Kathy's staying with the in-laws. Ella will be glad,
too. You always help her so nicely with her Latin.'

Beatrice woke as the sun, not yet visible, began to
lighten the cloudless sky. She was out of bed, had
washed her face, got into an old cotton dress she kept
for cleaning out the chicken house, tied back her hair
and was in the kitchen within minutes. Knotty was
waiting, and together they left the house and started
to climb the hill. Knotty had bounded on ahead, and
Beatrice, almost at the top, looked up to see why he
was barking.

She wasn't alone on the hill; Dr Latimer was there
too, waiting for her.

CHAPTER TWO

BEATRICE gaped, half a dozen questions rushing to her tongue.

'Later,' said Dr Latimer. 'Let us watch the sunrise first.'

They sat side by side with Knotty panting between them, while the sky in the east turned pink and gold, and the sun rose slowly between the distant hills. Only when the whole of its shining splendour was visible did Beatrice speak. 'You don't live here...?' And then, 'But it's only just gone five o'clock.'

'Miss Moore told me that you had returned home, and I knew that you would be here.'

How did he know? She let that pass for the moment. 'Miss Moore—do you know her? She's gone as companion to Great-Aunt Sybil.'

She turned her head to look at him, sweeping her hair over her shoulders out of the way. 'Did you tell her about the job?'

He said placidly, 'Yes. She is a retired ward sister who worked for me for several years. Not quite ready to sit back and do nothing much—it suits her to live with your aunt for the time being. She will be able to save every penny of the salary she gets—and I must admit that I found it remarkably poor. She intends to share a small house with a widowed sister, but it won't be vacant for some months.'

'She seemed awfully capable.'

'Oh, indeed she is.'

He sat back with nothing more to say, and presently she asked, 'Have you a day off?'

'No, but no patients until noon. Do you suppose your mother would give me breakfast?'

'I'm sure she will. There's only Ella home, and unless Father's been called out he hasn't a surgery until half-past eight.'

'You're glad to be home?'

She nodded. 'Oh, yes. I don't think I'm cut out to be a companion...'

'You have no ambition to take up a career?'

She shook her head. 'I suppose that years ago, when I was eighteen and full of ideas, I would have liked to train as a vet, but Father taught me a great deal and I like helping him. Ella's too young, and anyway she's not made up her mind what she wants to do, and Carol—she's the brainy one and works in an office, and Kathy will be getting married in a month.' She was silent for a moment, then, 'I'm almost twenty-seven, a bit old to start on a career.'

'But not too old to marry?' He paused. 'I feel sure that you must have had several opportunities. Dr Forbes did mention that his son and you...'

'People make things up to suit themselves,' declared Beatrice crossly. 'James and I have known each other forever, but I have no wish to marry him. I keep saying so, too.'

'Very tiresome for you,' agreed her companion, and gave her a kindly smile, so that her ill humour went as quickly as it had come. 'We had better go if we want breakfast...'

They went unhurriedly down the hill with Knotty cavorting around them, and so to the village and her home, carrying on a desultory conversation and on the best of terms with each other.

Early though it was, the village was stirring; Beatrice called cheerful good mornings as they went, not noticing the smiling, knowing looks exchanged behind her back. She was liked in the village, and although no one had actually said so it was generally thought that she was far too good for Dr Forbes's son. Her companion, aware of the glances, gave no hint of having seen them, although his eyes danced with amusement.

Mrs Browning was breaking eggs into a large frying pan on the Aga, and bacon sizzled under the grill. She looked up as they went into the kitchen, added two more eggs and said happily, 'Good morning. I do hope you've come to breakfast—such a satisfying meal. A lovely day again, isn't it? Beatrice, make the toast, will you? Ella's finishing her maths, and your father will be here directly.' She dished the eggs expertly and put them to keep warm. 'Are you on holiday, Dr Latimer?'

'I only wish I were. I must be back in town by noon...'

'Good heavens! All that way.'

'I had a fancy to watch the sunrise.'

He took the knife from Beatrice and began to slice the loaf, and Mrs Browning, bursting with curiosity, sliced mushrooms into the frying pan, reflecting that he couldn't possibly have driven down from London in time to see the sunrise, in which case, he must have spent the night somewhere nearby. After breakfast, when everyone had gone, she would phone the Elliotts... Lorna would surely know something about him. But her curiosity wasn't to be satisfied; when everyone was out of the way Mrs Browning phoned her friend, only to discover that she was on the point of going out and had to leave the house on the instant. Mrs Browning put down the receiver with something of a thump.

Beatrice, helping her father with his morning surgery, was wondering about Dr Latimer too; it was two hours' hard driving to get to London, and he had said that he had patients to see at noon. There had been no sign of a car; he must have had one, though, parked somewhere nearby—or did he live close by?

She had to hold a large, very cross cat while her father gave it an injection, her thoughts far away so that her father asked mildly, 'Will you take Shakespeare back, my dear? Mrs Thorpe will be waiting for him... I want to see him in two weeks, so make an appointment, will you?'

She bore Shakespeare away to his doting mistress, made an appointment in her neat hand and went back to the surgery where a small boy was standing, clutching a pet rat. She didn't care for rats or mice, but years of helping her father had inured her to them. All the same, she shuddered slightly as she took the animal from its anxious owner. There was nothing much wrong; advice as to diet and a few words of encouragement, and the small boy went away happy to be replaced by Major Digby with his Labrador. Since he and her father were old friends, a good deal of time was spent in talking about the good fishing locally, the chances against Farmer Bates planting sugar beet instead of winter greens and the vagaries of the weather. Beatrice, aware that she was no longer needed, left the two gentlemen, tidied the waiting-room and went along to the kitchen, where her mother was putting a batch of loaves to rise.

'I wonder where he lives?' she asked as Beatrice walked in.

'I have no idea, Mother. London, I would suppose, since that was where Great-Aunt Sybil went to see him. Probably he likes driving long distances.'

Beatrice spoke rather tartly, and Mrs Browning gave her a quick look.

'Oh, well,' she observed, 'we aren't likely to see him again.'

She was wrong. It was exactly a week later that Mr Browning had a heart attack—very early in the

morning, on his way back from checking Lady
Lamborne's pet donkey. Beatrice, coming down to
make early morning tea, found him lying at the
kitchen door. He was conscious, but cold and
clammy and a dreadful grey colour, and when she
felt for his pulse it was fast and faint. She wasn't a
girl to lose her head in an emergency; she put a cush-
ion under his head, covered him with the old rug
which was draped over one of the Windsor chairs,
told him bracingly that he was going to be all right
and went to phone Dr Forbes, fetched her mother and
then went back to crouch beside her father.

Dr Forbes was there within ten minutes, listened
to Beatrice's calm voice, examined his old friend and
told her to ring for an ambulance. 'We'll have to go
to Salisbury,' he told Mrs Browning. 'I'll give him
an injection and we'll keep him on oxygen.' He patted her arm. 'I think he'll do, but it's hard to tell for
the moment. Thank heaven that Beatrice found him
when she did.'

'You stay with him while I put some things in a
bag for him,' said Beatrice. Her voice was quite
steady, but her hands shook. 'You'll go with him?
I'll stay and sort things out here.'

She was back with the bag within minutes, and
urged her mother to get what she needed, ready to
go in the ambulance. Her father was quiet now, but
he looked so ill that she felt sick with fright, although
nothing showed of that upon her pale face. She held
one limp hand in hers, and stared down at her father,

oblivious of everything else, so that she didn't see Dr Latimer get out of his car at the same time as the ambulance drew up.

A large, gentle hand on her shoulder made her look up. 'Tell me what has happened, Beatrice.' His voice was calm and matter of fact, so that she answered him readily.

'Father—I found him here—Dr Forbes says he's had a coronary thrombosis.' She saw the ambulance for the first time. 'He's to go to Salisbury. Mother's going with him.'

Her voice had been steady enough, only it didn't sound like hers.

Dr Forbes had been talking to the ambulancemen; now he came to his patient. He paused when he saw Dr Latimer. 'We've met,' he said at once. 'You gave a talk at the seminar in Bristol last year... Latimer— Dr Latimer, isn't it?'

He launched into a brief description of Mr Browning's collapse, and Dr Latimer said, 'Do you mind if I come to Salisbury and take a look? I know Dr Stevens, we were students together...'

'I'll be glad of your advice—I suppose Dr Stevens will be in charge of him?'

'Oh, yes, but Mr Browning is a friend...'

He bent down and plucked Beatrice on to her feet to make way for the ambulancemen with their stretcher. 'Beatrice, find your mother, will you? I'll drive her into Salisbury; we'll get there ahead of the ambulance. Will you stay here?'

She said in a wispy voice, 'I must let several people know—farmers, mostly. The small stuff I can manage on my own... Will—will you telephone me if you go to the hospital with Father? I expect Mother will want to stay there.'

'As soon as we know what's happening I'll give you a ring, but stay here, Beatrice, until you hear from me.'

She nodded and went upstairs to find her mother. Mrs Browning, usually so matter of fact and competent, had gone to pieces for the moment. Beatrice took off the pinny she was wearing, got a jacket from the wardrobe, found her handbag and shoes and tidied her hair. 'Dr Latimer is here, he's driving you to the hospital so that you'll be there when Father gets there. He knows the consultant there too, so Father is going to get the best possible care.'

Her mother gave her a blank look. 'Your father's never been ill in his life. It's like a dream—a bad dream.'

Beatrice agreed silently and led her downstairs. The ambulance was just about ready to leave, and Dr Forbes was getting into it to be with his patient. Dr Latimer was waiting patiently at the door, and as they reached him Beatrice said urgently, 'You will let me know?'

'Yes. Come along, Mrs Browning.' He put an arm round her shoulders as he smiled at Beatrice and walked to the dark grey Rolls-Royce parked to one side of the drive. He opened its door and urged Mrs

Browning inside, got in himself and, with a wave of the hand, was gone.

Beatrice went slowly inside. There was a great deal to do, but just for a minute she was bewildered by the speed of it all, and the suddenness. It was a blessing that Ella had spent the night with a school-friend, but she would have to let Carol and Kathy know. As she went into the house, Mrs Perry, the elderly woman who came each morning to help in the house, caught up with her.

'I saw an ambulance, Miss Beatrice. 'as one of them dogs bitten your dad?'

'Dogs?' Beatrice gave her a blank look. 'Dogs—oh, no, Mrs Perry, my father has had a heart attack. My mother has gone with him to the hospital.'

'Oh, you poor love. I'll make a cuppa, it'll pull you together. And don't you fret, he'll be fine—them doctors are clever old fellows.'

She bustled into the kitchen and Beatrice went along to her father's study and opened his appointments book. Miss Scott, who acted as his receptionist-cum-secretary, would be in presently, but in the meantime there were several people expecting him that morning—farmers mostly. They would just have to get hold of another vet.

She began to telephone, drank the tea Mrs Perry brought her, and went along to the surgery. Her father's practice was mostly widespread among the estates and farms round the village, but there was always a handful of family pets needing pills or in-

jections and occasionally a stitch. The small patients
in the surgery now were easily dealt with, and she
attended to them with her usual calm; she had helped
her father for years and no one thought of disputing
her skill. The last patient, old Miss Thom's elderly
cat with ear trouble, was borne away, and Beatrice
put the surgery to rights, tidied the waiting-room and
started off towards her father's study. Miss Scott
would be there by now and she would have to talk
to her. The phone ringing stopped her, and she raced
back to the waiting-room and snatched up the receiver.

The voice at the other end sounded reassuring and,
at the same time, bracing. 'Beatrice? Your father's
in intensive care and is holding his own nicely. Don't
leave the house, I'll be with you in half an hour.'

He rang off before she could say a word. Just as
well, as she found that she was crying.

She felt better after a good weep, and with a
washed face, well made-up to cover her red nose and
puffy eyelids, she went to find Miss Scott. That lady
was sensible and middle-aged and could be relied
upon to cope with any emergency, and she was sorting the post, bringing the books up to date and going
through the appointments book. She looked up as
Beatrice went in, and said with real sympathy, 'I'm
so sorry, Beatrice—what a dreadful shock for you
all. Your father will be all right, of course; he's very
fit and he'll have the best of care. Mrs Forbes told
me that Dr Latimer has been called in for consulta-

tions—a splendid man, it seems. How fortunate that he happened to be here.'

For the first time Beatrice paused to wonder why he had been there, anyway. 'He phoned a few minutes ago. Father's holding his own. I waited to phone Carol and Kathy and Ella...'

'Quite right, my dear. You'd like to do it now? I'll go and have my coffee with Mrs Perry.'

Carol and Kathy took the news with commendable calm, and both said at once that they would come home just as soon as they could arrange it. Ella wasn't easy; Beatrice spoke to her headmistress first, so that she was half prepared to hear Beatrice's news. All the same, she burst into tears and demanded to come home at once.

'Of course you shall,' promised Beatrice, 'just as soon as I get some kind of transport. Be a good girl, darling, and try to be patient, just as Father would expect you to be. I'll ring you just as soon as I've fixed something up—there's rather a lot to do.'

Her sister's voice came, penitent in her ear. 'Sorry, Beatrice. I'll wait and not fuss. But you won't forget?'

'No, love.'

Miss Scott came back then and they set to work ringing round neighbours and neighbouring vets, fitting in the patients already booked by her father. They had almost finished when Dr Latimer joined them.

Beatrice jumped to her feet. 'Father—how is he?'

'Holding his own, as I told you; if he can hang on a little longer, he'll be out of the wood.' He bade Miss Scott a polite good morning and Beatrice introduced them. 'We're handing over most of father's patients for the moment—I've dealt with the minor stuff in surgery this morning.' She lifted unhappy eyes to his. 'I'm not sure what we should do...'

'Get a locum,' he told her promptly. 'Your father will need an assistant for a few months. I know you do a great deal to help him, but it will have to be someone qualified if he's to keep his contacts with the local farmers.'

She could have hugged him for his matter-of-fact acceptance of her father's recovery. 'Of course, I'll get in touch with the agency he uses sometimes—if he's on holiday or something...'

She smiled for the first time that day, and Dr Latimer studied her unhappy face without appearing to do so. 'Your father will be in hospital for a week or two, and when he's home he won't be able to do much for a time. Do you know of anyone he might like to work for him?'

She shook her head. 'No. They've always been different, and they've never been here for longer than three weeks.'

'Well, see what you can do. Get him here for an interview; it may make things much easier if you like him. Did you ring your sisters?'

'Yes. Carol and Kathy are driving back, they should be here quite soon. Ella's at school; I promised her I'd fetch her as soon as I could. I dare say Carol will fetch her.'

'Where does she go to school?'

'Wilton…'

'We'll go and get her now, shall we? Perhaps I should explain things to her…'

'Oh, would you? She's got her exams, and Father was anxious that she should pass well; if she could be reassured it would help a lot.'

Sitting in the soft leather comfort of his car, she said rather shyly, 'You're being very kind, and I'm most grateful. I know Mother will be too when she knows. You do think Father will be all right? Dr Stevens is very good, isn't he? Did he think he would recover?' She stopped and the bright colour washed over her face. 'Oh, I do beg your pardon, you're much cleverer than he is, aren't you? I mean, you're very well-known—Mrs Forbes said so. I expect Dr Stevens does what you suggest, doesn't he?'

A small sound escaped Dr Latimer's lips. 'Well, more or less—we pool our knowledge, as it were; he was good enough to allow me to take a look at your father. Is your Miss Scott reliable? Could she be left for a couple of hours while I take you to the hospital? Your mother wants to stay the night, and asked me to fetch some things for her. There is no reason why all of you shouldn't see him for a moment.'

'Thank you, I know we would all like to do that. But don't you have to work? Don't you have patients in London and hospital rounds and—and things?'

He said gravely, 'I take an occasional day off.'

'Oh, yes, of course. If you turn down the next street, the school's half-way down.'

Ella was waiting, red-eyed and restless. When she saw Dr Latimer she rushed to him and flung her arms around him. 'It's you. Oh, I'm so glad, now Father will be all right. How did you know? Had you come for breakfast?'

He didn't answer her questions, but said cheerfully, 'I'm going to take you to see your father, but first Beatrice has to put a few things together for your mother. She will stay at the hospital for a day or two while you help Beatrice to look after the house and the animals.'

He stowed her in the seat beside him and Beatrice got into the back, relieved at the placid way in which he had dealt with Ella, and once they were back home again he exhibited the same placid manner with Carol and Kathy, prevailed upon Miss Scott to stay until they returned, piled them all back into the car and drove back to Salisbury. And Beatrice sat in front beside him, listening to his advice, given in a diffident voice but sound none the less, so that, when he suggested that it might help if he were to be present when she interviewed any applicant for the post of assistant at the surgery, she agreed without a second thought.

'And it should be as soon as possible,' he reminded her, 'so that whoever comes has settled in nicely before your father returns.'

'I'll phone as soon as we get home,' she promised him. 'How shall I let you know if someone comes for an interview?'

'I'll leave you my phone number.' He drew up before the hospital entrance and they all got out. Ella was crying again, and he paused to mop her face. 'Your father is on a life-support machine, so there are a number of tubes and wires attached to him; don't let that frighten you. And you may only stay a few moments. Come along.'

Mrs Browning was sitting on a chair outside intensive care; she looked as pale as her daughters, but gave them a cheerful smile. She looked at Dr Latimer then. 'I'm eternally grateful,' she said. 'I don't know what we would have done without your help. And I do believe you when you say that Tom is going to get better.' She gave him a sweet smile. 'May the girls see him?'

'Certainly. Two at a time, I think. I'll just make sure that they won't be in the way...'

He disappeared, to return presently with a white-gowned Sister. 'Carol and Kathy?' he suggested. 'You'll have to put on white gowns. Sister will show you.'

They were only gone for a minute or two, and then it was Beatrice's and Ella's turn. 'And not so much as a snuffle from you,' warned Dr Latimer, giving Ella a gentle push.

Beatrice had steeled herself to see her father's grey face once more, but despite the tubes and wires he

looked more like her father again, with colour in his
face, and apparently asleep. The sight of him acted
like a tonic upon her; he was alive and he was going
to get better. Dr Latimer had said so. She quelled a
great desire to burst into tears, and urged Ella back
into the waiting-room.

Dr Latimer went away presently, excusing himself
on the grounds of a brief consultation with Dr Stevens, leaving them to drink coffee a nursing aide had
brought them.

They said goodbye to their mother when he returned, and he drove them back to Hindley, to share
the sandwiches which Mrs Perry had made and write
his phone number down for Beatrice, with the re-
minder that she was to phone him as soon as she had
an applicant to be interviewed. He wished them all
a cheerful goodbye, and for Beatrice at least the
house seemed very empty when he had gone.

But she had little time to sit and be sorry for herself; the most pressing necessity was for someone to
carry on the practice while her father was away.
While her sisters scattered to do the various jobs
around the house, she went to the study, found the
address of the agency her father had always used and
phoned them.

It had been a miserable day so far, now lightened
somewhat by the news that there was a newly qualified vet on their books who might be exactly what
Beatrice was looking for. An appointment was made

for the following day, and she went to find her sisters and tell them the good news.

'If he can come straight away, we shan't need to hand over too many of father's regular accounts. I can manage the surgery for a few more days, and we'll just have to go on as usual. I expect Mother will come home as soon as Father is out of danger.'

She spoke with a confidence she didn't feel, although Dr Latimer had told her with quiet certainty that her father would recover.

Dr Latimer phoned again around teatime; Mr Browning was showing a steady improvement, their mother would stay the night at the hospital, but if everything was satisfactory in the morning she would return home by lunchtime. 'Everything all right your end?' he wanted to know.

'Yes, oh, yes, we're managing. There's someone coming from the agency tomorrow morning, about eleven o'clock.'

'I'll be with you before then.' He hung up with a brief goodbye.

Tired out with anxiety and worry, they all slept soundly, but Beatrice was up soon after six o'clock, to let Knotty out into the garden, feed the cat, Wilbur, and make a cup of tea. Perhaps it was too early to ring the hospital, she decided, and then changed her mind, knowing that she wouldn't be content until she had news of her father.

He was continuing to improve, said Night Sister; they hoped to take him off the life-support machine very shortly, and perhaps Beatrice would like to telephone later in the day.

Beatrice drank her tea and set about the day's chores. There were several cats and dogs convalescing behind the surgery; she attended to them, fed Knotty a dish of tea and the bread and butter he fancied for his breakfast, and then went to wake the others.

Breakfast was almost a cheerful meal. 'I'll wait and see Mother,' said Carol, 'and then if everything is all right I'll go back—I can go straight to the hospital if—if I have to.'

'And I'd better go back, too,' decided Kathy, 'but you'll let me know at once if I'm wanted?'

Beatrice looked at Ella. 'You'd better go to school, love—Father will be disappointed if you don't do well in your exams. Yes, I know you don't want to— supposing we wait until Mother gets here and I drive you back in time for this afternoon's paper—biology, isn't it? Father would be so proud if you got good marks for that.'

Beatrice was clearing away after surgery when her mother arrived, and with her Dr Latimer. Her mother kissed her and said quickly, 'Oliver brought me back—such a good man and so clever. Your father's going to be all right, and we have Oliver to thank for that. He'll stay if you want him to just to cast an eye over this locum you've arranged to see.'

'You didn't mind me seeing to that, Mother? We

must keep the practice going well until Father can take over once again.'

'I'm only too thankful that you were here to deal with everything.'

She turned round as Dr Latimer came in with her case, and Beatrice said, 'I'll get Mrs Perry to bring in the coffee; there's still half an hour before that man comes.'

She smiled at him and thought how tired he looked—she had thought of him as a youngish man, but he looked pale and lined in the morning light. She was too worried about her father to bother much about the doctor; she went off to the kitchen and laid a tray while Mrs Perry made the coffee and got out the biscuits. By the time Beatrice got back, the other three were there as well as Miss Scott, and since everyone had a good deal to say and a great many questions to ask no one noticed that the doctor was rather quiet.

The doorbell interrupted them. 'You go, dear,' said Mrs Browning. 'You know as much about the practice as your father. Do what you think best.'

By the time Beatrice had reached the front door, Dr Latimer was beside her. 'The study?' he asked, and went there while she went to the front door.

Worried though she was, she couldn't help but be pleasantly surprised by the sight of the young man on the doorstep. James Forbes was young, too, but thick-set and slow and pompous; and Dr Latimer, regretfully, seemed a lot older than she had at first

thought. This man was splendidly different. She
blushed faintly at allowing her thoughts to stray so
frivolously. Guilt made her voice stiff. 'Mr Wood?
Will you come in?'

He smiled at her, self-possessed and charming.
'Miss Browning? The agency did explain...' They
shook hands and she led the way across the hall to
her father's study, where Dr Latimer stood looking
out of the window.

He turned round as they went in, and she introduced them. 'Please sit down, Mr Wood—would you
like a cup of coffee?'

'I stopped in Salisbury, thanks.' He glanced
quickly at the doctor, who met his look with a bland
one of his own. 'I understand your father needs a
locum for a month or two. I'm planning to go to
Canada in the near future, so perhaps we might suit
each other.'

He smiled at Beatrice, who smiled back; he was
really rather nice and they might get on well
together... She explained about the practice. 'I have
been helping my father for several years; I'm not
trained, but I do a good deal round the surgery and
help with operations.'

He asked all the right questions and she had time
to study him. He was good-looking, with dark hair
curling over his collar, pale blue eyes and a delightful
smile. She found herself hoping very much that he
would take the job.

Dr Latimer had said almost nothing, and she

thought pettishly that he might just as well not be there; he was certainly giving her no advice. Not that she would have taken it; when Colin Wood suggested that he might start in two days' time, she agreed with a readiness which made the doctor raise his eyebrows, but since she wasn't looking at him that escaped her notice.

Only as she was explaining the working hours and when he might expect to have some free time did the doctor ask gently, 'References?'

'Oh, of course.' Colin Wood shot him an annoyed look, and turned it into a smile as Beatrice looked up. He fished in a pocket and produced an envelope which the doctor took from him before Beatrice could do so. He read the small sheaf of papers closely, murmured, 'Entirely satisfactory,' and handed them back again. 'Were you thinking of a contract of any sort?' he asked casually.

'That won't be necessary,' said Beatrice sharply, 'if we have a gentleman's agreement.' She looked at Colin Wood. 'You are prepared to work here until my father can manage without help?'

'Oh, of course,' he said easily, and laughed. 'There, I've said that before a witness—what more can you want?'

'Would you like to see over the clinic?' offered Beatrice. 'And your room—there's a small sitting-room you can have, too.'

He rose with alacrity. 'May I?' He turned to Dr

Latimer. 'I'll say goodbye, sir. I'll have to go straight back and pack my things.'

They didn't shake hands; the doctor bade him a grave goodbye and stood watching them from the window as they crossed the wide sweep of gravel to the surgery on its far side.

Presently he went back to the drawing-room where Mrs Browning was sitting with the three girls.

'You approve?' asked Mrs Browning.

'He has excellent credentials and, what is more important, Beatrice likes him. He can come in two days' time.'

'You'll stay for lunch?'

He shook his head. 'I would very much like to, but I want to take another look at Mr Browning before I go back to town. But I'll be down again and I will keep in touch with Dr Stevens.'

'You'll wait to say goodbye to Beatrice?'

'Will you do that for me? I'm glad that things have been settled so quickly.' He shook hands and within a few minutes had driven away; a few minutes later Beatrice came in with Colin Wood, who was introduced to them all before saying that he simply had to go but looked forward to seeing them again in a couple of days.

Beatrice saw him away in his showy little sports car, and went back to her mother and sisters.

'Where's Dr Latimer?' she asked, and in the same breath, 'Well, did you like him? I think he'll be splendid—'

'Oliver,' said Mrs Browning gently, 'has gone back to check on your father's condition, then he is driving up to London, presumably to work at one of the hospitals. I only hope that he gets a rest during the day; he was up all night...'

'All night? Oh, I didn't know; that must have been why he was so quiet.'

Her mother said drily, 'Probably. You're satisfied that Mr Wood will do all right, darling?'

Beatrice nodded. 'Oh, yes, Mother. I'm sure he will, and he doesn't want a contract or agreement or anything in writing; he plans to go to Canada in a few months and wouldn't want to stay anyway. He says there aren't many good openings for a man without capital. He's ambitious.'

'I didn't like him,' said Ella suddenly.

'Why ever not?'

'I don't know—I just didn't like him.'

'Well, that doesn't really matter, for you'll not see much of him.' Beatrice spoke with unusual tartness. 'There's the phone—Father...'

It was Dr Stevens. 'Your father is recovering well, phone here for news some time in the evening. There is no need for your mother to come again today; she needs a rest anyway. Dr Latimer will be down to see him tomorrow afternoon. I suggest your mother comes then, and she can talk to him then about your father.'

'I'll tell her. Thank you for all you are doing, Dr Stevens.'

'It's Dr Latimer that you should thank—we had a very anxious few hours during the night, but he dealt with the complications. He's a very sound man, you know; you were lucky to have him.'

'We are very grateful,' said Beatrice, and put down the receiver slowly. Of course they were grateful, and she felt suddenly guilty because, in the pleasure of meeting Colin Wood, she had forgotten the doctor.

She did her best to make up for it the following afternoon. She and her mother had visited her father, who was conscious now and feebly cheerful, and then they were ushered into Sister's office, where Dr Latimer and Dr Stevens were murmuring thoughtfully together. They turned impassive faces towards them as they went in, shook hands and offered chairs.

'Well,' began Dr Latimer, 'your husband is coming along very nicely, Mrs Browning, but it will be a slow job—you do realise that? We'll keep him here for a week or two, and when you get him home he will have to take things easily for some time.' He smiled then, and Beatrice thought once again what a very nice man he was.

She said, 'We are truly grateful to you, Dr Latimer. We can never repay you...'

'My patient's recovery is payment enough, Beatrice,' he told her coolly, and for some reason she felt snubbed, not by his words but by his manner—perhaps in hospital he was impersonal to everyone, but he wasn't the man who had watched the sunrise with her on Midsummer's morning, or if he were he was taking care to hide it.

She accompanied her mother back home, and after they had all had tea Carol left to go back to her rooms in Salisbury and Kathy went off with her fiancé. 'In the morning you can go back to school, Ella,' said Mrs Browning. 'The house will seem empty.'

'Mr Wood will be here,' observed Beatrice, and felt a little surge of excitement.

CHAPTER THREE

COLIN WOOD arrived the following morning with a great deal of luggage, several tennis rackets and a set of golf clubs. He was charming, too, and offered to start work at once.

'Well,' said Beatrice, 'I must say that's nice of you—I saw to morning surgery—there wasn't anything I couldn't manage by myself, but Mr Dobson— he has a big farm a mile or two down the road— wants someone this afternoon. He's not quite happy about a cow due to calve. I told him you might be here in time to go.'

'Splendid, that gives us time to go through the appointments book. I'll unpack, shall I?'

He breezed away to his room and Mrs Browning watched him go with a faint frown. 'He's very—very self-assured...'

'A good thing, Mother dear. We must keep this practice going until Father can get back.' She gave her parent a comforting hug. 'And he will be; this morning's report was very reassuring. I'll get the coffee, then Mr Wood and I can get down to the books.'

She went to bed tired that night, but satisfied with the day. She had driven her mother to the hospital that afternoon, and there was no doubt that her father

was better. When they got home again it was to find
Mr Wood back from the Dobson's farm, sitting at
her father's desk in the surgery, checking the appointments for the evening surgery. He had had tea
with them but hadn't sat over it, declaring that he
wanted to go through the files and get to know as
much as possible quickly. So Beatrice had joined
him, showing him as much as she could before surgery started, and then stayed with him to give him a
hand with the ease of long competence. And after
supper she spent half an hour with him while he
looked over the next day's appointments.

She closed her eyes, happier than she had been for
several days. Colin Wood was the perfect answer to
their difficulties; what was more, she liked him.

The days fell into a regular pattern again: morning
surgery, outside calls, taking Knotty for his walk,
helping around the house and taking her mother to
see her father each afternoon, and then evening surgery and more work, going through the next day's
appointments. Her father's practice was a large one,
and scattered, and she could see now that he would
have to have a partner or at least an assistant other
than herself—indeed, he should have had one months
ago, for although she acted as his right hand she had
no qualifications. She began to hope that when
eventually her father came home he would take to
the idea of keeping Colin Wood as his partner.

Dr Latimer had come to see them, arriving quietly
just as they had finished the afternoon clinic; he

didn't stay long. 'Mr Browning is doing very well indeed,' he told Mrs Browning. 'Another week or ten days and you will have him home again, although you do understand that he must do very little? But there is no reason why he shouldn't do some desk work if he feels like it.'

He had smiled kindly at Mrs Browning, and added, 'Of course, Beatrice and Mr Wood will bear the bulk of the work for the moment.'

Beatrice said quickly, 'Of course, Colin has taken everything over without a hitch.' She glanced warmly at the young man, and the doctor watched her without appearing to do so.

He said placidly, 'I'm sure you must feel very grateful to Mr Wood. I take it that everything goes smoothly with your father's practice?'

Beatrice beamed at him. 'Oh, yes, thank you.' And then, feeling that she should show some interest in him as well, 'Are you very busy? Would you like to stay for supper?'

'I should like very much to stay,' he told her, 'but I must get back to town this evening; I never quite catch up with my work, I'm afraid.'

Colin Wood laughed. 'You need someone to organise you, like Beatrice, sir. She keeps my nose to the grindstone...' He smiled across the room at her. It was full of charm, and held a hint of possessiveness.

The doctor got up to go. 'I shall be seeing Mr

Browning in a few days' time; I hope I shall have good news for you then.'

He bade Mrs Browning goodbye, nodded to Beatrice and Colin Wood and went away, accompanied by Mrs Browning.

'Seems a nice enough old boy,' said Colin when they had gone. 'A bit slow, but I dare say he's good at his job.'

Beatrice said sharply, 'He's not old, and he's quick enough when someone's ill...'

Colin gave her a quick glance. 'I'm not criticising him; he's quite famous, isn't he? I must say he's been wonderful in his care of your father.' He added contritely, 'I shouldn't have said that he was old—he's not. Somewhere in his thirties, I should suppose.' He smiled disarmingly and she forgave him at once. She liked him; that was, she liked him almost all the time. Sometimes he said or did something which struck a note of doubt in her mind, but she forgot that quickly enough. He was beginning to fill her thoughts, so much so that James, when he had encountered her in the village, had been given short shrift and told once and for all that she had no wish to marry him.

'I've been saying so for months,' she told him reasonably, 'but you never would listen. But I do mean it, James. We wouldn't suit, you know you don't really love me. It's only because we have seen each other on and off for years and years. And there isn't anyone else, so you don't have to mind...'

He hadn't minded all that much, either, and she

felt free at last. Free for what? she asked herself, and immediately thought of Colin.

He was very efficient and he wanted to know as much as possible about the practice. Indeed, one morning after surgery she had gone into her father's study to fetch something and found him sitting at the desk, looking through the accounts for the previous year with a neat summary made by Miss Scott showing just what the income for the year had been.

She had shown her surprise, and he had said quickly, 'I wanted to look up the treatment for Mr Gregg's pigs—I seem to have got hold of the wrong file.' He gave her an apologetic smile. 'Sorry about that, but there is rather a lot to cope with all at once...'

Her sudden feeling of suspicion faded. 'That's all right; I think you're managing beautifully. It must be very difficult, taking over at a moment's notice. The treatment files are on the second shelf. You'll find the pigs under G—Miss Scott is a wizard at keeping things in order.'

'It's a large practice, too,' he observed as he put the file back. 'I can't think how your father managed on his own; there's work enough for two at least. Of course, he had you, and I must say you're as good as any vet.'

She pinkened delightfully and shook her head. 'But not qualified. When he's home again he will have to have someone besides myself.'

He said lightly, 'Well, I might decide that I don't

want to go to Canada, after all.' He smiled. 'There's
more than one reason why I might want to stay.' He
was looking at her very intently. 'A man wants to
settle down, you know. I thought that I was footloose
and fancy free, and Canada for a year or so seemed
the answer, but now I'm not so sure.'

She didn't pretend not to understand him; it never
entered her head to do so. Her colour deepened, but
she returned his look honestly.

'You have only been here a week or so. It's too
soon for you to decide anything.'

He had crossed the room and taken her hand.
'Dear Beatrice, some things don't need deciding—
they just happen.'

She had lain awake that night for quite some time
thinking about him. She had her daydreams like any
other young woman, now she was allowing them free
rein. Colin liked her, perhaps more than liked; what
could be better than a partnership with her father?
The practice would stay in the family, they could live
nearby, and when her father retired they could stay
on in the house and her parents could move to a
smaller house in the village. It was almost too good
to be true. She allowed common sense to take over
for a moment. She wasn't quite sure that her feeling
for Colin was anything stronger than liking; he attracted her, she liked to be with him and she thought
about him a lot, but she was still uncertain. She had,
naturally enough, fallen in love several times, but she
had fallen out of it again without either pain or re-

gret; she wasn't, truth to tell, quite sure how one was certain that one was in love. She had always imagined that one was quite sure with not a single doubt, but at the back of her mind she had to admit to herself that there were vague doubts she couldn't put a finger on. Perhaps, she decided, on the edge of sleep, one was never absolutely sure...

The days slid into a week, and then two, and her father was coming home again. Dr Latimer had been to see them again, confident that her father would be almost as good as new, provided he took things easy.

'And no worry of any kind,' he advised. 'No accounts or finance for the moment, and don't let him get tired. He can advise from his desk, see patients if he wants to, provided that there is someone to do the actual work. But no night calls or sudden emergencies. I'm sure you and Mr Wood will be able to arrange that between you.'

He was in the drawing-room, sitting opposite Beatrice and her mother. 'He's settled down nicely?' He looked at Mrs Browning.

'Yes.' Mrs Browning sounded hesitant. 'In fact he seems to have taken over completely, if you know what I mean, although I'm sure that's just my fancy.' She glanced at Beatrice. 'Beatrice tells me that he's splendid in the job, and I'm sure we're very lucky to have him.' She paused. 'Only I hope that when Tom gets back home Colin will understand that he will want to take charge again...he behaves rather as though the practice is his.'

Beatrice frowned. 'I think you're worrying about nothing, Mother.' She spoke gently, but there was an edge to her voice. 'Colin wouldn't dream of usurping Father's place.'

She looked at Dr Latimer and found his intent gaze fixed on her and went red. 'I don't know what we should have done without him,' she spoke defensively. 'I like him—we get on very well.'

She looked away crossly because Dr Latimer was smiling and the smile held mockery.

He went presently with the promise that he would examine Mr Browning at the hospital three weeks later. 'Dr Stevens knows everything there is to know; if you're at all worried, let him know, he will deal with any problem and Dr Forbes is close by. I think that you have no further need to worry, provided Mr Browning takes care.' He shook hands. 'And remember, no worries or sudden surprises.'

Two days later Mr Browning came home, looking almost as good as new. Dr Forbes called almost as soon as he was home, checked that he hadn't suffered from the journey, advised him to go slow for a week or two, and told him to be sure and call him if he were needed. On the way out, he stopped to speak to Beatrice. 'I'm sorry that you and James...' He coughed. 'Known each other all your lives; rather took it for granted...'

She came to his rescue. 'That's why,' she told him gently. 'We're more like brother and sister, you know; James will realise that when he meets the right girl.'

'I'm sure you're right, my dear; I hope that you meet the right man, too.'

Beatrice was almost sure that she had, but she wasn't going to say so.

Colin was a tower of strength during the next few days. Indeed, she thought worriedly, too much so, for her father was inclined to be irritable at Colin's assumption of so much of the practice. At least, it wasn't so much that he had shouldered the major share of it, it was his satisfied air at taking everything upon his shoulders... She longed to tell him this, but she was afraid that if she did he might resent it and leave; something which was the last thing she wished for. He was beginning to fill her life and her thoughts, and it worried her that no one else shared her opinion of him. True, her mother was unfailingly polite and thoughtful for his comfort, but Ella made no secret of her dislike of him, and after the first few days it was only too apparent that her father, while agreeing that he was very good at his job, had no liking for him. This was something which Colin smoothly ignored, for he never mentioned it to her and she had to admire him for that; indeed, in her eyes, he could do very little wrong. He was always charming and kind to her, letting her know in a dozen ways that she mattered. She wished that there was someone who would lend a sympathetic ear to her worries. Dr Latimer would have done very well, she reflected, only he seemed to have disappeared into his own particular busy world, and when her father would go to hospital for an examination, even if he were there, there would be no chance to talk.

But she had her chance. A week or so after her father had returned home, she came in from feeding the animals convalescing behind the surgery, and found him sitting in the garden, stretched out in one of the garden chairs, talking to her father. It was a warm day, and she had been up early to attend to a litter of puppies before she had started on her usual chores. She was hot and tired, her nose shone and her mane of hair had come loose of its plait. Over and above that, her father had been annoyed because Colin had altered a treatment which he had been in the habit of using for years. Life was getting complicated, and now here was Dr Latimer, looking cool and immaculate and faintly amused.

She wished him good morning in a cross voice, which he chose to ignore. 'Busy?' he asked unnecessarily. 'And on such a lovely day, too. Have you been up the hill lately?'

'I haven't had the time.' She bent to pat Knotty's head as he sat by her father. 'Have you come to see Father?' She frowned at his amused look. 'I mean, to examine him?'

'No, that will come in a week's time. Besides, he looks pretty fit to me. I was coming this way and I had half an hour to spare.'

They had had coffee; she longed for a cup herself

and said, still cross, 'It's a lovely day, as you said. I dare say you will be gone before I get back…'

'You have surely finished for the morning in the surgery?' asked her father. 'We always had half an hour to ourselves before I did my rounds. I see no reason to change my ways—'

Dr Latimer interposed smoothly, 'Come back here when you've done your hair or whatever; we might take a stroll. You look as though you need a little time to yourself.' He met her vexed look with a placid blue stare, so that she found herself agreeing…

She felt more in tune with her world when she had done her face and brushed her hair. She ran down to the kitchen and drank a glass of lemonade her mother was making, and, much refreshed, went into the garden again.

'That's better,' observed Dr Latimer. 'Shall we go and look at the world from the top of the hill? Knotty is dying for a walk. So is Mabel.'

'Mabel?' Beatrice just stopped herself in time from asking who is Mabel? She followed him out into the lane. His wife? A small daughter? A girlfriend? Not possible, he would never have left them sitting in the car.

Mabel, she discovered as they reached the car, was an amiable Labrador, lolling on the front seat by the open window.

'Oh, why didn't you bring her in?' cried Beatrice.

'She hasn't met Knotty, and they might have romped around and disturbed your father. Besides, she rather fancies herself guarding the steering-wheel...'

He let the dog out and Mabel was made much of before trotting off ahead of them with the amiable Knotty at her heels. The doctor strolled along in a comfortable silence, and Beatrice's ill temper left her. They had begun their climb up the hill before he asked, 'Something's wrong? Tell me about it.'

It seemed the most natural thing in the world to unburden herself to him, and it all came out in a muddle of doubts: her father's scarcely concealed antipathy towards Colin, Ella's frank dislike. 'And it's all so unfair,' she mumbled. 'He works so hard—you have no idea...' The doctor, who had a very good idea of what hard work was like, merely made a soothing sound, and she went on, 'He manages so well, he's even gone through the books with Miss Scott. She didn't want him to, but he said he had to know as much about the practice as possible.'

'The books? You mean the appointments and the various cases?'

'Oh, those too—no, the account books. Just to get some idea, he explained; he's very conscientious...'

'And you like him.' It was a statement, not a question.

She said defiantly, 'Yes, I do—he's—he's young and alive and he's—well—fun.'

'Of course,' the doctor's voice was just sufficiently sympathetic. 'I dare say he's ambitious too.'

'Oh, yes—he wants his own practice, but of course

he's only been qualified for two years and he hasn't the capital.'

Dr Latimer was surveying the landscape below them. 'He's young enough to work for that,' he commented, 'and he'll be the better for it.'

She agreed doubtfully; Colin wasn't a man to wait for what he wanted, but it seemed disloyal to say so.

The silence between them lengthened, until she said slowly, 'I did wonder if Father would make him a partner...'

The doctor's gaze was still on the scenery. 'It's early days yet,' he counselled. 'Give him time to—er—er—discover Colin's worth.'

She said gratefully, 'You're such a nice person to talk to. I've been wanting to talk to someone; I can't worry Mother, Ella's too young—besides, she doesn't like Colin—and Kathy and Carol aren't at home.' She added quickly, 'I don't want advice...'

'Regard me as an uncle or an elder brother—I'll promise never to advise you, Beatrice. But for what it's worth, I'll listen.'

She gave him a grateful look. 'Thank you. I think I'm a bit muddled.'

'Things have a way of sorting themselves out,' he pointed out comfortably. He whistled to the dogs. 'I would like to stay longer, but I must get back to town.'

'To the hospital?'

They started down the hill with the dogs racing

ahead. 'I have an out-patients session this afternoon...'

She asked, for something to say, 'You don't work in the evenings?'

'Sometimes.' He smiled. 'This evening I'm giving myself the pleasure of dining out.'

'Is she pretty?'

He cast her a sidelong glance. 'Yes, extremely so.'

For some reason his answer annoyed her: she said pettishly, 'Oh, that's nice; I dare say she has lots of time to buy lovely clothes and have her hair done...'

His smile was instantly suppressed. 'Indeed, yes. She is one of the lilies of the field—neither toils nor spins.' He added blandly, 'She dances delightfully.'

'Then I expect you will have a simply wonderful time.' Beatrice spoke with something of a snap.

They were turning into the drive and she said, 'I must check on Mrs Sim's cat; there should be kittens some time today.' She stopped and held out a hand. 'Thank you for letting me talk. It must all seem very petty to you after your life and death work.'

'No. Life is never petty, Beatrice.' He put up a finger and gently tapped her cheek. 'I hope the kittens arrive safely.'

He went on towards the house, leaving her feeling that she had had something taken away from her.

But she forgot that almost at once. Mrs Sim's Siamese was about to produce her kittens and Beatrice stayed with her until four tiny creatures were tucked up against their proud mother, who squinted at

Beatrice and purred her delight before accepting the
milk and chopped liver she was offered. By the time
Beatrice got back to the house there was no sign of
Dr Latimer. She hadn't expected him to be there; all
the same, she felt disappointment, quickly forgotten
when Colin got back from his visit to an outlying
farm.

The afternoon clinic was short; she cleared up after
it, and since there was an hour or so in which there
was little to do she suggested to Colin that they might
go for a walk.

'My dear, I have a mass of paperwork to get
through—Miss Scott overlooked some accounts, and
I'm trying to sort them out.'

'Accounts? That's not like her.' Beatrice leaned
over the desk and took a look. 'Oh, you don't have
to bother about those—Father won't send those in
for a few months—Bruton's Farm had bad luck with
their sheep this year and the bill is enormous; they'll
pick up again, but they've got to live in the meantime. And these—' she sorted through a handful
'—they're all smallholders who are only just beginning to make things pay. They won't get their accounts for another six months.'

She picked up the small sheaf of papers and put
them tidily back on the shelf.

Colin frowned. 'But that's not the way to run a
successful practice; if they use the vet, they must pay
for him.'

'And so they do, the moment that they can afford to.' She added coolly, 'It's Father's practice, Colin.'

He got up from behind the desk and came to stand by her. 'My dear girl, I had no intention of interfering. I'm sorry—I wanted to help.'

He smiled at her apologetically and she forgave him at once; she was half in love with him, she supposed, and it was difficult to resist his charm. She said, 'That's all right—come and see the kittens. They're a nice little bunch. Mrs Sims will be delighted—she relies on breeding them to help out her pension.'

She forgot, or almost forgot, the small episode, and a week went by like most weeks; plenty of work mitigated by her father's rapid recovery and glorious weather. Kathy's wedding was only a few days away, and the whole house was in cheerful turmoil, with Mrs Perry polishing and helping out in the kitchen, a marquee erected in the garden and a great deal of toing and froing by the ladies of the household, trying on their wedding outfits and experimenting with hair-styles. But somehow they managed to create a quiet oasis around Mr Browning, who was left to sit peacefully in the garden or his study. He was beginning to take an interest in the practice once more, and expected Colin to see him each day so that they might discuss the various animals to be seen and treated. And outwardly, at least, Colin appeared to welcome this, although several times he changed the treatment Mr Browning had ordered and did what he

wished to do. He was careful not to let this be
known, and since he was a good vet no harm came
to his patients, but he derived satisfaction from edg-
ing his way deeper and deeper into the practice. Another few months and he hoped Mr Browning might
accept him as a partner, even though he had no
money to put into the practice. In the meantime he
was pleasant to everyone, worked hard and remained
the best of friends with Beatrice.

The weather held, and Mrs Browning's secret
nightmare, that it might rain on the wedding day and
spoil all her careful arrangements, melted before blue
sky and bright sunshine. The caterers arrived, the
wedding cake was carefully set on its stand and the
bouquets were delivered.

Beatrice had got up earlier than usual; wedding or
no wedding, the animals needed attention. She had a
hurried breakfast in the kitchen and went to her
room, poking her head round Kathy's door as she
went.

Kathy looked beautiful, and Beatrice said so before tearing off to have a shower and get into her
bridesmaid's dress, which was of pale rose wild silk,
the long skirt veiled with chiffon, the bodice quite
plain, the ballooning sleeves ending at the elbow in
tight bands. It was a style which suited Carol and
Ella as well as herself. She took pains with her hair,
winding it into a chignon and fastening the little
wreath of silk roses around it. Surveying herself in

the pier glass in her mother's room, she hoped that Colin would approve...

There were a lot of guests; the Brownings had lived in the village for several generations and they were liked; besides, Kathy's bridegroom came from a large family. The village church, half-way up the main street, was packed with best summer dresses and morning-suits with a fair sprinkling of villagers in new hats and stiff white collars. Beatrice, with Ella and Carol, waiting in the porch for her sister and her father to arrive, was gratified to see that all those who had the use of their legs had come to watch the bride go to her wedding.

Kathy looked a little pale, but her father looked remarkably well as they went up the path to the church. Beatrice rearranged her sister's train and followed them up the aisle, and a whisper of sound went through the church at the sight of the four pretty girls, quite serious now, looking ahead of them to where the bridegroom stood. However, Beatrice allowed her eyes to wander to the pews on her family's side, looking for Colin. He was there, well turned out, quite sure of himself—and standing beside him was Dr Latimer. She hadn't expected that; true, she hadn't sent out many of the invitations for she had been busy for the greater part of each day, but no one had said that he would be a guest. But there he was, rather larger than life on account of his great size, wearing his morning coat as though he were in the habit of doing so frequently—and it was certainly not hired from Moss Bros, Beatrice reflected as she glided slowly past the pew, for it fitted to perfection. He turned his head and looked at her, and she felt her cheeks pinken most annoyingly. They were at the altar now, and she realised that she hadn't looked at Colin at all; she must remember to smile at him as they left the church.

She did, smiling into his rather sulky face and ignoring the doctor, and once they were back at the house she wandered around the marquee, greeting friends and family, and edged her way to where he was standing. If she had hoped for a compliment about her appearance, she was to be disappointed; she didn't know why he was so sullen, it was a side of him she hadn't encountered, and she asked him, without mincing matters, what was the matter. 'It's Kathy's wedding. You should at least look as though you were enjoying yourself...'

He caught her hand. 'Oh, my dear, I'm sorry. You see, I've been sort of wishing that I was the bridegroom, and you...' He paused and smiled. 'I mustn't say more, not yet.'

And in any case he hadn't the chance; an elderly uncle Beatrice hadn't seen in years appeared at her elbow and marched her off to have what he called a cosy little chat, and which lasted until it was time to toast the bridal pair. It was then that he disappeared from her side and Dr Latimer took his place, a glass of champagne in each hand. He offered her one, and said, 'Hello, Beatrice. You look very fetching in that pink thing.'

She thanked him gravely. 'I didn't know that you would be here.'

'No—well, I don't suppose it would have made much difference if you had. When do we hear the next peal of wedding bells?'

She took a sip of champagne. 'I don't know what you mean,' she observed coldly.

'Don't be coy. Not ten minutes ago you and young Wood were holding hands.'

'I'm not coy,' she snapped, and then, 'I liked it—having my hand held.' She smiled at him. 'I'm sorry if I snapped. You have always been so kind to all of us, and I'm very glad you could come today.'

'So am I. Kathy is a beautiful bride and they look very happy. Your father has stood up to all this very well. I've asked him to Salisbury tomorrow, and I'll have a look at him before I go away.'

'Away? Where to? For a long time?'

He smiled faintly. 'I have a short lecture tour: Paris, Brussels and the Hague. I shall be gone for a week.'

She beamed her relief. 'Oh, that's all right, then—I—we all feel safe about Father while you're looking after him.' She added frankly, 'I had no idea that you were so important. Dr Forbes was telling me.' She smiled suddenly. 'Have you seen Great-Aunt Sybil?'

'Oh, yes, indeed. She addressed me as "young man", which did a great deal for my ego.'

'I shouldn't think your ego needed anything done for it—oh, Father's going to make a speech...'

She didn't speak to him again, only exchanged a brief goodbye as he left later. And as Dr Forbes had said that he would drive her father into Salisbury since he had to go there himself, she wouldn't see Dr Latimer there; she was aware of a vague regret about that.

Her father came back the next day feeling very pleased with himself. He had passed Dr Latimer's meticulous examination with flying colours, and provided that he was sensible there was no reason why he shouldn't take on the less heavy work of the practice.

'What I shall do,' he observed to Beatrice and her mother, as they sat in the drawing-room after supper, 'is get hold of an older chap; he can deal with the night work and the more distant farms until I'm up to it again. There's that empty house at the other end of the village—it belongs to Forbes, and he wants to rent it out, not sell it. It would do nicely for a man with a small family.'

Mr Browning puffed at his pipe and looked pleased with himself.

'What about Colin?' Beatrice made her voice casual.

'I'll give him a month's notice—he's a locum and he came on that understanding, did he not?'

'He's worked very hard,' persisted Beatrice. 'He knows a great deal about the practice.'

'Good experience for him. I'll see him in the morning.'

Beatrice went to bed presently, but not to sleep. Somehow she had taken it for granted that Colin would stay on, perhaps as a partner. The future, still vague in her mind, had been full of exciting possibilities, and it had suddenly become empty. She got up early and took Knotty for his walk before having her breakfast and plunging into her busy day. The house was still in a state of upheaval after the wedding; there were things to pack up and return, the caterers to collect the leftovers, a posse of men to take down the marquee. No one had time to speak to anyone, and since Colin had been called out to an injured horse Mr Browning had no opportunity to talk to him.

They met at lunch, all of them edgy from the excitement of the wedding and its aftermath of muddle, and no one talked much, but as they got up from the table Mr Browning said, 'Colin, will you come to my study? There is something I should like to discuss with you.'

Colin jumped to his feet, smiling, and Beatrice thought how boyish he looked and how willing he was to please. The two men went away and she started to clear the table and carry the dishes to the kitchen for Mrs Perry to wash. Colin, she felt sure, would be able to persuade her father to let him stay. She wandered off to one of the paddocks to cast an eye over the old donkey abandoned by a party of tinkers. His hoofs were in a sorry state, but good food and rest would give the beast a new lease of life. Her father had accepted him without demur, knowing that he would never be paid for his treatment, and she remembered with a small frown that Colin had voiced the opinion that the donkey should have been turned over to the RSPCA, or failing that, sent to the knackers. Then, seeing her look of horror at his suggestion, he had made haste to tell her that he was only joking. He had caught her hand, smiled into her eyes and told her that she was soft-hearted and that he loved her for it.

She did her usual afternoon chores, made sure that everything was ready for the early evening clinic and went along to the surgery. Colin was there, sitting at the desk, writing. The face he turned to her was, as usual, smiling. 'There you are. When you are not around I feel lost! Come and sit down; I've almost finished this letter. What a bore all this paperwork is…'

'You should let Miss Scott do it; she knows everything about the practice and she's marvellous at letter-writing.'

'Oh, I like to keep my hand in.' He put his pen down. 'It's such a glorious day. Do you suppose we might sneak off for a walk after tea?'

Her heart sang. 'Why not? I've seen to the sick animals and got the surgery ready—we could spare half an hour. Father wanted to see Dr Forbes's dog and he's the first case.'

So after tea, a rather silent meal in the drawing-room, she accompanied Colin across the paddocks and into the narrow lane running behind the garden. At first they talked trivialities, but presently Colin took her arm. 'You know, Beatrice, we get on awfully well, don't we? We're friends?' And, when she nodded, 'I'd like it to be something more than that—I've nothing much to offer, but I intend to make my way to the top in record time. I'll not say any more now, that wouldn't be fair, but think about it, darling—you're everything a man could want, and so beautiful.'

Before she could speak, he added, 'Don't say anything, just remember what I've said.'

And he began to talk about the good results he had had from a new drug he had been using on a nearby pig farm.

Beatrice passed the next week or two in a state of dreaminess, interlarded by vague doubts which she couldn't put a name to but which persisted at the back of her mind. Her father had said nothing more about Colin going, and she hadn't asked. Surely if Colin had been going to leave he would have told her? She allowed herself to dwell in a state of euphoria and ignored the niggling doubts.

Which made it all the more nightmarish when the doubts became certainty. Pure unlucky chance had sent her back to the surgery after the short afternoon session. Colin had told her that he was going out to one of the farms, her father was resting and her mother was in the kitchen with Mrs Perry, making jam. Beatrice went unhurriedly across the garden which separated the surgery from the house, intent on collecting the towels they had used. The door to the surgery was open and she walked in, her sandalled feet making no noise, and stopped doubtfully when she heard Colin's voice. He was on the phone, and the door to the office was half-open. She took a step forward to see why he was still there and then she heard her name.

'Beatrice? I've got her eating out of my hand. No, I haven't told her I'm going; I've a couple of weeks still, time enough to persuade her to marry me—her old man can't do much if his daughter marries me, can he? Only offer me the partnership.' He laughed. 'Oh, she's OK. Not my type, but I can't have everything, can I?'

He was silent, apparently listening to someone at the other end of the phone, and Beatrice stood like a statue, her world slowly tumbling around her, not quite believing her ears. A great wave of humiliation seemed to sweep over her, doused by indignation and rage as he spoke again, 'I've been through the books—it's a first-class practice, plenty of lolly; I shan't be able to get my hands on it at once, but after a few months, once we're married, I'll get my besotted Beatrice to hand some of it over.'

He laughed again. 'No, I'm not a rogue, just a man with an eye to the main chance. Besides, she thinks I'm the only man in the world...'

Beatrice had been frozen to the spot, now suddenly she turned and sped out of the door, running blindly to get away. She had no idea that the tears were streaming down her face, and she couldn't have cared less if she had known. She could hardly believe it, and she couldn't see where she was going, so when she ran full tilt into Dr Latimer, she let out a breathy yelp and tried to pull away from him.

He caught her neatly and made no effort to let her go. 'Dear, oh, dear.' His voice was disarmingly gentle. 'No, don't talk for a moment. Let me mop you up, and then presently you shall tell me all about it.'

CHAPTER FOUR

BEATRICE choked, sniffed and allowed him to dry her sopping cheeks, but presently she took the handkerchief from him, blew her nose in a no-nonsense fashion and mumbled, 'Could we go away from here—please?'

He flung an arm around her shoulders, where it lay as solid as an oak and just as heavy but strangely comforting. 'My car. I've only just driven up, no one knows I'm here—we'll go for a drive.'

He drove unhurriedly through the narrow lanes, going towards Tisbury and then tooling around the maze of still narrower lanes; no distance from Hindley, but to all intents and purposes buried in remote country.

'Nice here,' he observed. 'Restful and delightfully green.'

Beatrice sat quietly beside him, his hanky screwed up in a wet ball in her hands, and she said politely, 'Yes, it is lovely. You know your way around here; but of course, you stay with the Elliotts, don't you?'

He didn't answer directly. 'I know them very well.'

They had come to a widening in the lane and a gap in the trees on either side of it. He stopped the car. 'A pity there's a hill in the way, otherwise we would get a splendid view of Wardour Castle.'

She turned obediently to look, and heard his gentle sigh. 'And now, are you going to tell me what happened?'

'No—oh, no,' said Beatrice, and instantly contradicted herself. 'He wants the practice—I heard him telephoning. I didn't mean to eavesdrop, but the door was open and I heard my name.' She gave a sniff. 'That's why he was looking through the books, but he said he'd got them off the shelf by mistake. Father's getting a partner and Colin is to go, and I thought...he said—he said that he could easily get a partnership if he m-married me, only he doesn't love me.'

The doctor sat quietly beside her, sorting out her mutterings and making sense of them. He asked quietly, 'Did Colin tell you that he was leaving?'

'No. And Father didn't either. I asked Father if Colin couldn't stay as his partner, but he wants an older man, only I thought that Colin—he said that he hoped he could stay and I... I've been such a fool, haven't I?'

'No. You may feel one, but you aren't one. If he gave you to understand that he was in love with you and hoped one day to marry you, you had every reason to believe him.'

'But he was only pretending because he knows Father's practice is a good one, and it would have been so easy for him to take over in time and have all the benefit of Father's hard work without having done much towards it himself. He wanted the money, I suppose.' She gave a shuddering breath. 'I thought he wanted me.'

She hadn't looked at the doctor once, which was just as well, for his usually placid expression had been replaced by a look of ferocity, but his voice was as calm as usual. 'And how fortunate that you discovered that he didn't before any harm was done. Just think, if you hadn't heard him just now, you might possibly have married him and been unhappy ever after.'

She said in a woebegone voice, 'Yes, I'm sure you are right. But I don't know what to do.'

'Do? Why, behave as though you know nothing of this conversation of Colin's. Of course, he will—er—make overtures of a romantic nature; but fore-warned is forarmed, my dear, and I'm perfectly certain that you will be able to deal with those as they occur.'

'Oh, will I?'

'But of course—all women have an inborn instinct for frustrating a man in his intentions. I have no doubt that you are well equipped to do this just as well as any other.'

He watched her reluctant smile and said, 'That's better. You're hurt and upset, but believe me, you will get over it, although that's cold comfort now, isn't it? But you have your father to think of as well—on no account must he be worried or bothered.

Can you carry on as usual, do you suppose? You have become very friendly with Colin, have you not? Perhaps there is rather more than friendship on your part?' He took no notice of her quick breath. 'He goes in two weeks, doesn't he? Not long, and you're a level-headed girl, not given to hysterics.'

'I don't feel at all level-headed at the moment,' declared Beatrice in a tear-clogged voice.

He turned to look at her, his blue eyes impersonal, just as though he were examining a patient. 'Not quite your usual self, perhaps,' he conceded. 'If I drive you back, can you manage to get to your room and repair the damage?'

Sensible advice, and yet she found herself wishing peevishly that he wasn't quite so sensible.

She said with something of a snap, 'Yes, of course.' And after a moment, 'Thank you for listening to me and giving me advice. You're quite right, and I'll do what you suggest.'

He started the car again. 'If you need help, give me a ring. You know my London number, and if I'm not there I can be reached.'

'You're very kind. It's only two weeks...'

Not long, but how she dreaded them.

Back at home, he opened her door. 'Off you go,' he urged her. 'I'm going to see your father and mother, and no one need know that I arrived half an hour ago.' He gave her an encouraging pat on her shoulders and she said goodbye and ran indoors. No one was about, and she gained her room and spent twenty minutes getting her face back to normal. Only then did she go back downstairs, to meet Dr Latimer in the hall, bidding her mother and father goodbye. His suave, 'Ah, Beatrice, how are you? I'm so sorry that I have to go just as we meet again,' disconcerted her for a moment.

However, after only a tiny pause, she said in her usual calm way, 'Oh, I'm sorry, I was in my room cleaning up after seeing to the kittens. But you'll be down again? Are you pleased with Father?'

'Yes, indeed I am, but no excitement or exertion, from what he tells me he is doing enough for the moment.'

He smiled at her, shook hands with her mother and father and drove himself away.

'So good of him to call,' said her mother. 'He seems to come this way a great deal. Perhaps he visits someone...he's not engaged, is he? I mean, he could be coming to see a fiancée, couldn't he?' She looked at Beatrice. 'I know he doesn't stay with the Elliotts, not lately, anyhow. I wonder where he goes?'

'I dare say he has other friends than the Elliotts, Mother; he might even have other patients in this part of the world.'

'Yes, dear. Oh, Colin popped in to say that he'd gone over to Muston's Farm, and if he's not back could you get the clinic organised?'

Beatrice bent to pat Knotty. 'Yes, of course. Fa-

ther, did you want to see Dr Forbes's dog again?
He's due for another injection.'

Her father nodded. 'Yes—I'll take the clinic too.
There aren't many booked, are there?' And, at her
questioning look, 'Dr Latimer suggested that I should
do so and see how I felt.'

She wouldn't have to see Colin again then until
the evening. She sighed with relief.

He was at supper, of course, entertaining them
with a light-hearted account of his visit to Muston's
Farm, and at the end of it suggesting that Beatrice
might go over the patients booked for the next day.
It was something they had done several times, sitting
in the clinic, discussing each case at length and finding time to talk about other things as well. But this
evening that was something Beatrice just couldn't do.
She made the excuse that she had several phone calls
to make to friends, and a letter she simply had to
write to a friend who had gone to live in Canada.

Immediately she had said that, she worried that
Colin might think it strange, for she had been more
than willing to go with him on several occasions. She
would have been furious if she had known that he
wasn't in the least put out; his conceit allowed him
to suppose that it was because she was shy of him
since he had allowed her to see his supposedly real
feeling for her.

It was her mother who remarked upon it as they
were clearing the table after supper. 'Are you sure

you didn't want to go with Colin, dear? You usually do.'

And at breakfast the next morning Mr Browning, who had got up early, remarked, 'Beatrice, when Mr Sharpe—Mr Cedric Sharpe—comes this morning, about ten o'clock, bring him to my study, will you?' At her questioning look he went on, 'He sounds very suitable as a partner, but of course we need to talk about it.'

Beatrice couldn't stop herself looking at Colin, but he was looking down at his plate. 'Colin is going in rather less than two weeks,' went on her father. He looked across at his assistant. 'I dare say you will find Canada rather different from here.'

Colin looked up. 'I'm not sure that I'm going,' he said. His smile was disarming. 'In fact, I have great hopes of staying in England.'

He looked across at Beatrice as he spoke and, mindful of Dr Latimer's advice, she smiled back rather vaguely and said, 'Oh, really? I feel sure there are plenty of jobs going.'

The morning clinic was busy, and she was kept hard at work, but, when the last four-legged patient had been borne away and she began on the clearing up, Colin strolled over to where she was washing instruments.

'Are you wondering why I didn't tell you that I was leaving?'

She made her voice as non-commital as possible. 'Well, no, I wasn't. You were only a locum; I knew you would be going as soon as Father felt he could get back into the practice.'

'With a partner.' He sighed loudly. 'That was a bitter blow to me, Beatrice. I had hoped that he would offer a partnership to me. I know I have no capital, but I have brought a lot of up-to-date ideas into the practice, and eventually I could have taken over completely.'

Beatrice began to lay out clean towels. 'Oh, I don't think Father would ever retire; he's not all that old, you know, and he'd die of boredom. I dare say you would do much better in Canada—there must be an enormous scope for vets out there.'

Colin came a little nearer, and she whisked away to the sink and began to wash the bowls they had used.

'You must know why I want to stay.' He sounded so sincere that if she hadn't listened to his conversation on the phone she would have believed him. 'We get on so well together, Beatrice, you can't pretend that you don't know how I feel...'

It was fortunate that the phone rang then, for it saved her from having to answer him. She pounced on the instrument like the proverbial man clutching at a straw, and said 'Hello,' so heartily that Dr Latimer at the other end observed softly in her ear, 'Am I right in thinking that I have phoned at exactly the right moment? In a tight corner, are you? Could you be free on Saturday? I'd like to take you out.'

'Oh, would you? How nice.' She was aware that

she sounded inane, but she had been taken by surprise. 'Why?' she asked.

'A whim—a breath of fresh air, preferably in company. I'll pick you up about nine o'clock.'

'I haven't said…'

'No. I know. I dare say Ella will do your chores
for you. Bring Knotty with you, if you like.'

She put down the phone and Colin asked sharply,
'Who was that?'

'A private call. I must go up to the house and see
if Mr Sharpe has arrived.'

He was on the doorstep as she reached the front
of the house; a stocky, middle-aged man with a mild,
craggy face and wispy, greying hair.

'Just right for Father,' muttered Beatrice, making
herself known and showing him indoors. She left the
two men together and went along to the kitchen to
make coffee for them. Her mother and Mrs Perry
were there, debating the advantages of a steamed jam
pudding over treacle tart for supper.

'He's here,' said Beatrice. 'Mr Sharpe. He looks
nice.'

'So Oliver says,' said her mother.

'Oliver? Who's Oliver?'

'Dr Latimer, dear. It seems silly to be so formal
with him, doesn't it?'

'Yes. Well, I suppose so. But how did you you
know about Mr Sharpe?'

'Oh, he recommended him to your father in the
first place.'

'Did he, indeed?' Beatrice assembled the coffee-tray and bore it to her father's study, and when she got back to the kitchen Colin was there, exerting his charm on the two ladies. He turned it on Beatrice as she went in.

'I was just saying how I shall miss you all when I finally go. I feel so completely at home here.' He pulled a wistful face. 'Life is going to be very empty.'

'Not if you get a job, it won't,' observed Beatrice cheerfully. It was surprising, she thought, how she could be so casual with him while all the time her heart was—if not broken—severely cracked. In a day or two, she was sure, when she had got over her indignation and shock, she would feel unhappy; she had been almost but not quite in love with him…and she had never doubted that he was attracted to her, had fallen in love with her. Hurt pride was a splendid thing to stiffen one's backbone.

After a day or two, she got rather good at keeping Colin at a distance. Several times he had hinted strongly that he couldn't bear the thought of leaving her, but she had never given him a chance to get any further than that, although it had been tempting to do so—just once, to see what he would say—but pride forbade her.

Her father had accepted Mr Sharpe as a partner, and it was no longer possible for Colin to put off his arrangements for leaving with only a week left before Mr Sharpe and his family moved into the house in the village. He had become reticent as to his future plans, hinting to Beatrice when they were alone that he had no intention of going out of her life. She took no notice of this; she was honest enough to know that she was going to miss him, although she despised him for his pretence. All she wanted now was for him to be gone.

Ella was perfectly willing to do Beatrice's chores on Saturday; she disliked Colin, but she was good with the animals. It was a pity that at supper on the Friday evening she should have remarked upon Beatrice's outing with Dr Latimer. Mr and Mrs Browning knew of it, but had remained discreetly silent, so that it was left for Ella to let the cat out of the bag.

'You'll have to put up with me in the morning,' she told Colin. 'Beatrice is having a day off—Dr Latimer is taking her off somewhere.'

Colin's face had darkened, and after a moment he pushed back his chair. 'I've just remembered a prescription I had to have ready,' he said to no one in particular. 'You'll excuse me?' He cast Beatrice a long, reproachful look as he went.

'Didn't he know?' asked Ella innocently.

It had rained overnight, but the sky was a clear blue when Beatrice got up the next morning. She spent a good deal of time going through her wardrobe; Dr Latimer hadn't said where they were going. How like a man, she thought, wondering whether a blue linen dress and a little jacket would be more suitable than a pale pink cotton dress with a demure collar. Ella, who had wandered in, eating an apple, said, 'Wear the pink; men like pink.' She added as she sidled across to the bed and perched on it, 'I'm sorry I let Colin know about you going out with Oliver—I didn't know he didn't know, cross my heart.'

'No harm done. Who said you could call Dr Latimer Oliver?'

'Well, Oliver did. Dr Latimer is so stuffy; he must get awfully sick of all the nurses bending the knee and calling him Dr Latimer with every other breath.'

Beatrice poked her head through the pink dress. 'I believe they call consultants "sir" in hospital.'

'Really? That makes him sound like a stuffed shirt, and that he most certainly is not.' Ella tossed the core into the wastepaper basket. 'I shall probably marry him when I'm grown up.'

'Does he know?'

'I don't think I'll even tell him, in case I meet someone I like better.'

'Sound thinking,' observed Beatrice, and started throwing things into her good leather handbag. 'I wish he'd said where we were going.'

'Well, you look all right,' said Ella kindly, 'and it isn't as if you're going out to dinner, is it? Will you be gone all day?'

'I don't know. He didn't say.'

'I expect you will go into Salisbury and have lunch in some stuffy restaurant.'

Beatrice gave her face a last-minute survey. 'He said he wanted a breath of fresh air.'

'A picnic on Salisbury Plain,' said Ella.

'I'd like that.' Beatrice went downstairs and found Colin in the hall, obviously waiting for her.

'If only I'd been free today,' he began in an aggrieved voice, 'we could have spent the day together. But I'll make up for it once I've left here.'

Beatrice wasn't paying much attention, for she had heard the doctor's car coming up the drive; it came to a whispering halt and she went to open the door, saying over her shoulder, 'Yes, you'll take a holiday, I expect.'

Dr Latimer had got out of his car and was strolling round to the kitchen door, but he stopped when he saw her.

'I didn't expect you to be ready,' he told her. 'I was going to say hello to your mother. I dare say your father is at the clinic.'

'Well, no—he'll be with Mother. It's Colin's Saturday duty.' She frowned as she spoke; he should have been in the clinic, seeing his patients, instead of mooning round the hall. The frown cleared when she heard Ella's voice shouting for him, her clear young voice raised impatiently.

'You've several patients and it's five past nine already.'

The doctor lifted an eyebrow, but continued on his way, although he spent barely five minutes with

Beatrice's parents before urging her, quite unnecessarily, to hurry up.

'But I've been ready for ages,' she protested, and
blushed at his,

'I'm flattered.'

In the car she asked, 'Where are we going?'

'Not far. Would it bore you to loll around in the
sun for an hour or so? And perhaps a swim?'

'It sounds lovely, but I haven't my swimsuit with
me.'

'Oh, I dare say one can be found for you.' He
began to talk in a pleasant rambling fashion about
nothing much, and she sat back and let all the small
worries of the week melt away. Colin had been very
tiresome once or twice, almost as though he were
quite happy to be leaving, and yet hinting that he
would still be able to see her...

'Only another five days,' said Dr Latimer suddenly. 'Has it been difficult?'

It was such a comfort to have her thoughts read.
'Yes. At least, I don't know why, but Colin makes
me feel uneasy; he behaves as though we shall go
on seeing each other even though he's leaving.'

'Does he, now? A pity you can't go and stay with
your great-aunt, but then you would have to leave
your father—your mother looks after him quite
splendidly, but I don't think she could cope with
young Wood, and your father must be protected from
anything likely to raise his blood pressure.'

'Oh, I'll be all right.'

They were on a country road she knew well, going in the direction of Phillip's House, a large estate only a few miles away, and she wondered where they were going, but she didn't like to ask again for he hadn't answered her the first time, only talked about swimming and lying in the sun.

They entered the village just short of the estate, and he slowed the car and turned down a narrow country lane, away from the few houses in its main street.

'There's a lovely old house along here,' said Beatrice chattily, 'with a red-tiled roof, and it's all shapes and sizes, just as though whoever lived there needed to add a room or so from time to time. I expect you've seen it?'

They were almost level with its open gate, and he slowed the car. 'Well, yes. I live here.'

She shot round in her seat to look at him. 'You do? I thought you lived in London.'

'Well, I do for a good deal of each week, but this is my home. It's been my family's home for a long time.'

He drew up in front of the solid door, undid her seat-belt and leaned across to open her door; and when she got out he put a hand under her elbow and ushered her into the house. There was an elderly man standing by the open door.

'This is Jennings—he and Mrs Jennings look after me.'

She shook hands, aware that a pair of very shrewd

blue eyes were studying her. Jennings' voice held
satisfaction. 'Welcome, Miss Browning.'

He stood aside to let them pass, and it wasn't until
much later that she wondered how he had known her
name—the doctor hadn't mentioned it...

The hall was wide, low-ceilinged and panelled; an
oak dower chest against one wall held a bowl of
roses, and against the opposite wall there was a solid
oak table flanked by two high-backed, cane-seated
oak chairs. There were flowers here too, and wall
sconces with pale rose-coloured shades. There were
doors on either side, and passages leading off left
and right with an uncarpeted staircase, its wooden
treads worn with age, at the back of the hall.

'In here,' said the doctor, and opened a door and
swept her before him. The sitting-room was low-
ceilinged like the hall, but with plain white walls
hung with paintings. There was a bow window at one
end with a window-seat beneath it, piled high with
cushions, and the fireplace was wide and deep. The
chairs and sofas were velvet-covered and looked
comfortable, and Mabel got out of one of them to
bounce across the floor and greet them. Beatrice bent
to pat her and took the opportunity to take a good
look around her. She liked what she saw; it was a
lived-in room despite the splendid glass-fronted cabinets along its walls, which were filled with porcelain
and silver, and the magnificent crimson brocade curtains at the window. The window-panes were latticed
and old, but at some time or other a door had been

made to open into the garden beyond. She wandered over to look through it and the doctor opened it.

'The garden's rather nice,' he observed. 'We'll go round it presently if you would care to.'

'Oh, I would.'

'Coffee first, though. Come and sit here and tell me how your father is.'

She thought for a moment. 'I think he's improving fast, especially now that he's arranged for Mr Sharpe to take up a partnership.' She hesitated. 'I think he will be glad when Colin's gone.'

'Can you tell me why?'

'I think he feels that he's being edged out, if you see what I mean.'

'And you, Beatrice? I understand that you will be glad to see Wood go, but perhaps in your heart you are hoping that there has been a misunderstanding. Have you spoken to him? Asked him to explain his conversation on the phone?' He paused. 'Let him see that you are a little in love with him?'

Beatrice raised her lovely eyes to his. 'I think I'd rather die,' she said quietly, which somehow made the words all the more dramatic. She went on. 'I—I shall miss him, and I think I've been hoping that he would explain, but he hasn't, because of course he doesn't know that I heard him in the first place.'

The doctor agreed gravely, a gleam of amusement in his eyes. 'Then things should be left as they are, don't you agree? He will be gone in another few days, and in time you will mend your cracked heart.'

This sensible speech cheered her up; they drank their coffee and presently wandered out into the garden. The grounds were large and beautifully laid out, and when they came to a high, old brick wall the doctor opened a wicket gate and ushered her into the kitchen garden with its rows of orderly vegetables, fruit bushes and raspberry canes. The walls were lined with apricot and peach trees, and there were apple and pear trees growing haphazardly between the beds of peas and beans and beetroots.

'Oh, this is fabulous,' cried Beatrice. 'It must be looked after by several gardeners.'

'Old Trott, who's been with us, man and boy, and his two grandsons, and I like gardening too when I have the time.'

They strolled around in the bright sunshine, and she felt happy for the first time in days—a gentle happiness, very soothing to her trampled ego and gently stoked by her companion's manner towards her: a well-balanced mixture of casual friendliness and pleasure in her company.

The swimming pool looked inviting, hidden away behind a screen of trees, with lounger chairs arranged invitingly around it. There were small changing-rooms at one end too, and the doctor said placidly, 'Mrs Jennings found some swimsuits; I dare say one might fit you. Shall we have a swim before lunch?'

There were half a dozen swimsuits in as many sizes. Beatrice, weighing the charm of a dark blue one-piece against the spectacular stripes of a bikini, chose the blue; it did more for her splendid figure than any bikini, but she hadn't thought about that.

The doctor was already in the water; she slipped in feet first and began a sedate breast-stroke, but by the time she had swum the length of the pool the warmth of the water and the bright sun encouraged her to alter her speed, and in no time at all she was racing her companion up and down its length until they cried a truce and got out to lie in the sun.

The doctor was an undemanding companion; Beatrice lay half asleep, speculating idly as to who else had a choice of the wonderful swimming-suits he had provided. It was a pity, she reflected, that she didn't know him well enough to ask. She turned her head to look at him, lying on the lounger next to her. He looked even larger in swimming trunks than he did in his formal grey suits; his eyes were closed and she felt a faint flicker of annoyance that he was actually asleep, but at least it gave her the opportunity of studying him at length. Very good-looking, but, now she came to notice, the good looks were etched with lines of weariness. Six feet, five inches at least, she guessed, and a pair of shoulders which wouldn't disgrace a prize fighter. She lifted her head a little in order to get a better view of his commanding nose, and then drew in her breath sharply when he opened one eye.

'How very discourteous of me. I had rather a disturbed night.'

'Why?'

'Oh, a patient I have been looking after.'

'You had to go to him in the middle of the night? I thought specialists didn't do that.' She frowned. 'Don't you have a registrar at the hospital?'

'Oh, yes, but specialists get up in the middle of the night too. It's all part of the job.'

'Do have another nap,' she begged. 'I'm very happy just lying here doing nothing.'

He rolled over to look at her. 'How nice of you to say that. But that would be a waste of time. Shall we dress? I'll show you the horses before lunch.'

'Horses? You ride?'

'Whenever I can. You do, too?' He had got to his feet and bent to pull her to hers. 'There's still half an hour before lunch.'

There were two chestnuts in the paddock beyond the kitchen garden, and with them an elderly donkey. They came to the gate and took the sugar they were offered, and Beatrice stroked their soft noses. 'Nice beasts—do you hunt?'

'No. I like to ride wherever the fancy takes me.'

'And the donkey?'

'Kate? Oh, happy enough to live here with the horses.'

'A pity there aren't any children to ride her...'

'Yes, but that can be remedied in the future.'

Beatrice had her mouth open to ask him if he was about to marry, but stopped herself just in time. 'She looks very fit,' she observed.

The doctor whistled to Mabel. 'Time we went

back for lunch. What would you like to do this afternoon?'

'Lie in the sun,' said Beatrice promptly, 'and you can tell me about your work.' They were strolling back towards the house. 'No, that wouldn't be fair. You must want to get away from it at weekends.'

He smiled a little. 'And you? What do you intend to do, Beatrice?'

'Me? Well, stay and help Father, I suppose...'

'And then?' he prompted.

She said uncertainly, 'I don't know; I suppose I haven't thought about it a great deal. That is—' She went pink, but turned her candid eyes on his. 'I suppose I thought that Colin would ask me to marry him.'

The doctor stared down at her. 'He probably still will do so.'

'But he's going...'

'He is leaving the practice, which is an entirely different matter.'

They had reached the house, and Jennings came to meet them. 'I've put drinks on the terrace, sir—if the young lady wishes to tidy herself, Mrs Jennings will show her the cloakroom.'

So Beatrice did her hair and her face and used the charming cloakroom beside the staircase; Ella had been quite right, the pink dress looked nice. Feeling light-hearted, she drank her sherry and listened to the doctor's placid voice talking about nothing in particular, and presently was led across the hall to the dining-room; it was panelled like the hall, and furnished with a rectangular table in mahogany and a beautiful bow-fronted sideboard. There were eight ribbon-backed chairs, but lunch had been laid at one end of the table and they sat facing each other, eating iced watercress soup, chicken salad and raspberries and cream, and drinking Chablis. Afterwards they went back to the terrace and had their coffee. Thinking about it later, Beatrice couldn't remember what they had talked about, only that she had enjoyed every minute of it.

And presently, stretched out on a swinging ham-mock in a shady corner of the garden, with the doctor lying on the grass beside her, she drifted off into a vague daydream, very much influenced by her sur-roundings. To be able to live in such a lovely house would be a delight in itself; she tried to fit Colin into the picture, but somehow he didn't seem right. She must forget him; perhaps if she went away for a week or two?

'I'll give two guesses,' murmured the doctor, his eyes half shut, watching her face. 'Colin...'

'Well, yes, partly. I can't help it, although I do try. It'll be all right once he's gone.' She rolled over in order to see him better. 'Oliver, it will be all right, won't it?'

'Of course. That is the first time you have called me Oliver.'

'Oh, is it? You see, most of the time I have seen you, you've been a doctor.'

'I see what you mean. Don't forget I am a friend as well, Beatrice.'

'I won't. Has Ella told you that she intends to marry you when she grows up? You'll be in the family.'

'A pleasant thought, but a pity that in another five years or so I shall be fortyish. I fancy she may have changed her mind by then. She's a nice child.'

'Haven't you any brothers or sisters?'

'Four sisters, all married with children, and a younger brother. He's a houseman up in Edinburgh, and just got himself engaged to a very pretty little nurse.'

'So you're the only one...' began Beatrice, and went red. 'Sorry, I didn't mean to pry.'

'Not married,' he finished for her. 'Although I rather fancy I shall achieve that state in the near future.'

She longed to find out more, but he began to talk about the garden and what he planned to do that autumn. Not quite a snub, but almost, she reflected while they discussed Christmas roses and chrysanthemums; she must take care not to let her tongue run away with her.

They had tea presently—sandwiches and fruitcake and tea poured from a silver teapot, all brought out to them by Jennings, with a strapping girl carrying a folding table to put everything on. Beatrice munched cake and reviewed a safe topic of conversation. 'Have you had your holiday yet?'

'In the spring. I went to Madeira; it's a splendid place for walking. It rather depends on various things as to when I shall take another week or two. And you?'

'Oh, I don't expect so. I'm hoping Mother and Father will go away somewhere quiet, just as soon as he feels that the practice is his, if you see what I mean, and that Mr Sharpe is able to cope. I'll stay at home and look after things. Ella is going on one of these school trips—climbing in Cumbria—and Carol is going to Paris to stay with some friends of hers.'

'So the house will be empty; you and Knotty will have time to climb the hill every morning if you want to.'

They went indoors presently, still talking in a desultory way while he showed her the library and urged her to roam the bookshelves and take anything she fancied. She settled for a history of Dorset, a very old edition, and a book on the Greek Islands.

He drove her home fairly soon after dinner, spent ten minutes or so chatting to her parents, smiled nicely at her when she thanked him for her lovely day, and a little to her chagrin didn't suggest that they might do the same thing again. But later, thinking about it, she had to acknowledge that, if he was intending to marry, his future wife might not approve.

Colin had been in the sitting-room when they had gone in, but he had greeted them with perfect good

humour, remarked upon the weather and took himself
off in a cheerful manner. Perhaps he had become
reconciled to leaving, after all, thought Beatrice, and
forgot about him while she recounted her day to her
mother and presently took herself off to bed feeling
happy. Although just before she slept she was conscious that behind the happiness was a tinge of sadness.

CHAPTER FIVE

BEATRICE managed not to be alone with Colin during the next few days, something made much easier by reason of her father's increasingly active part in the running of the practice. As yet, he spent only short periods at the clinic, but this meant that Colin had more visits to pay, so that he was seldom for any length of time at the clinics when they were held. And, when the actual day of his departure came, Beatrice was agreeably surprised that he made no mention of seeing her again, but bade them all a friendly goodbye, got into his sports car and drove himself away.

'I must say,' observed Mrs Browning, 'that I'm quite glad to see him go; your father wasn't all that happy about him. He did his work well, but there was always this feeling that he was encroaching, gradually pushing his way in. He did want a partnership, but he couldn't have expected one without some capital. Besides, he's young; a few years as an assistant won't hurt him.'

She took Beatrice's arm. 'I wonder when we shall see Oliver again. Such a busy man, but perhaps he'll find time to come and see us next time he goes to his home. So strange that he lives only a short drive away. His home must be lovely...'

'It is.' Beatrice was conscious of a great wish to see it again, although she very much doubted if she would. 'Would Father like me to go down to the village and make sure the house is ready for the Sharpes? They'll be here this evening, won't they?'

The next two or three days passed peacefully. Mr Sharpe proved to be exactly what Mr Browning wanted: unassuming, pleasant and hard-working. And, being a Dorset man himself, he was able to get on very well with the local farmers. Beatrice, helping at the clinics, found him easy to get on with too, and, although she missed Colin more than she had thought she would, it was a relief to return to the mundane way of life she had known before he came.

Only it didn't stay mundane for long. Towards the end of the week she had gone down to the village shop for her mother. The fine weather had broken and she had cycled there, wrapped against the weather, propped her bike against the wall outside the shop and gone inside. The shop was unusual in that it sold groceries which wouldn't have shamed Fortnum and Mason, and at the same time it did a nice line in knitting wools and local pottery; and since it was just across the street from the village's famous pub it did a splendid trade, especially in the tourist season. But today, since the weather was bad, the shop was empty, and Beatrice, having passed the time of day with the proprietor, took her time over choosing bacon and cheese and the kind of biscuits her father preferred. It was while waiting for Mr Drew to fetch the particular brand of chutney her mother wanted that she glanced out of the window. Crossing the road was Colin, making for the shop.

He came in quietly and shut the door behind him. 'Hello, Beatrice. I saw your bike. I thought you would be down sooner or later.'

'You're still here,' she said stupidly.

'Of course, and I don't intend to go until we've had a talk.' He came and stood close to her, and she edged away until her back was against the counter. 'There wasn't much chance before; you kept out of my way, didn't you? But you can't really have thought that I would just go without seeing you. Beatrice, I shall stay here in the village until you say that you will marry me; then your father will have to offer me a partnership. He's far too fond of you to let you marry a penniless man.' He put out a hand and laid it on her arm. 'And if he doesn't want me in the practice, he would give us the money to get started on our own.'

Beatrice struggled to find words. She lifted his hand from her arm, and said, 'I'm a means to an end, aren't I? Well, I shall say this once: if you were the last man on earth I wouldn't marry you; you're wasting your time. I suggest that you go away and find yourself a job—preferably on the other side of the world.'

Colin's smile turned ugly, but Mr Drew, coming

back with the chutney, gave her the chance to turn away from him and finish giving her order. She barely heard Colin's whispered, 'I shall stay here; don't think you can get rid of me so easily. After all, there's no one else, is there? You told me that once.'

She bitterly regretted that now as she cycled back home.

And he was as good as his word. Whenever she went to the village or took the dogs for a walk, he contrived to meet her; and after a day or two, when she reluctantly stayed away from the village and took the dogs in different directions, he wrote to her— impassioned letters, declaring his love and outlining a brilliant future for them both if she would marry him.

Oliver had said that her father wasn't to be worried, and that applied to her mother, who had worry enough; Carol was still away and Ella was too young; Beatrice said nothing to anyone, and began to look a little pale and worried, as well as becoming unusually short-tempered. When she wanted him, she thought crossly, the doctor wasn't there; there had been no sign of him for days. He could at least have phoned.

She came back from exercising the dogs, hot and tired and hardly at her best, and was putting the last of them back in its kennel when Oliver spoke from the door. She turned to look at him, not answering his cheerful 'hello' at once.

'Where have you been?' she wanted to know peevishly. 'It's almost a week...'

He said mildly, 'I've been over in West Germany—a consultation. What's the matter, Beatrice?'

She came out of the shed which housed the dogs and closed the door. 'I'm sorry I snapped. I've so wanted to talk to someone...'

'About Colin?'

'Yes. How did you guess? He's making a great nuisance of himself. I can't make him understand that it's quite hopeless expecting to—to marry me so that he can get a partnership. He's still in the village, at the Lamb. Whenever I go out, he's there.'

'How tiresome for you,' observed the doctor, and she said crossly,

'Of course it's tiresome; I hardly dare show my nose outside the clinic. What's more, there is no one to talk to about it.'

'There is now, I'm here.'

'Yes, but you'll go again as soon as you've seen Father, and I want to talk forever.'

'I've already seen your father. If you've finished for the time being, walk up the hill with me and tell me about it; I've nothing to do for the rest of the day.'

She looked down at her cotton dress. 'I'm not a bit tidy—my hair...'

'Looks perfectly all right, and who's to see, anyway?'

A bracing speech, but hardly flattering.

They walked in silence for some distance, but as they neared the summit of the hill she began, 'I don't know what to do. I'm so afraid that Colin will come up to the house and upset Father. Father knew that I liked Colin, I didn't make a secret of it; I even suggested that he might be made a partner—that was before—before...'

'You found him out. So that if he spoke to your father now, he might suppose that you were still in love with Colin.'

'Not in love,' she said quickly. 'Infatuated, I suppose, or at least only a little in love, but not any more. I'm suffering from outraged pride, and I'm scared that he'll do something to upset Mother and Father. How am I ever to convince him that I want nothing more to do with him?'

The doctor flung a large, comforting arm around her shoulders. 'There is a simple way of doing that. You and I, Beatrice, will become engaged.' She turned to face him, her mouth half open, her eyes wide, slow colour mounting into her cheeks.

'Before you utter a word, let me point out that I have not mentioned marriage, not even a proposal; but Colin wouldn't know that, would he? But if we let it be known that we are engaged, he will almost certainly realise that hanging around here in the hope of marrying you is a waste of his time; better by far that he should go in search of some other young woman with a comfortable background and good prospects.'

Beatrice's cheeks were their usual healthy pink, but she looked distinctly ruffled. 'It is very kind of you to offer,' she began haughtily, 'but I'm sure that's quite unnecessary. I'll think of something.'

The doctor wasn't in the least put out. 'You are a resourceful young woman, and I have no doubt that you will think of a great many ways of getting rid of him. When you've exhausted them all, my offer still stands!'

It was quite illogical of her to feel that he had let her down, especially when he started a cheerful conversation about Mabel, whom he had left at her father's house, enjoying a romp with Knotty. They had reached the top of the hill and stood side by side, looking at the wide spread of country before them.

'Is Germany as lovely as this?' asked Beatrice after a minute or two, searching for a safe topic.

'Parts of it, yes, but England is beautiful, and some of the best beauty spots are so hidden away that it takes a lifetime to discover them.'

He smiled at her as he spoke, so kindly that she said quickly, 'You're not annoyed because I don't want to be engaged to you?'

'Dear girl, of course not. I am rather too old for you in the first place, and in the second, we are not sufficiently good friends to cope with such a situation.'

'You're not in the least old, and you must know that we all regard you as a friend after what you have done for Father.'

'Too kind,' murmured the doctor. 'You forget that it is all in the day's work for me.' He glanced at his watch. 'Perhaps we should be strolling back? Your mother mentioned ham on the bone and potatoes in their jackets for supper.'

Soon, as they neared the house, she said quietly, 'Thank you for listening, Oliver. It helps a lot, doesn't it, to talk to someone…?'

'Oh, yes, and probably tomorrow you will find Colin gone and all your worries with him.'

But he was wrong there; buoyed up by the foolish idea that Colin might actually be gone because the doctor had suggested it, Beatrice went down to the village; there was Colin, strolling along, coming down the hill from the church, quickening his steps when he saw her. She was still some way away from the shop and there were no side roads, only grassy paths between some of the cottages. She walked on, and when they drew level wished him a cool good morning and made to pass him.

He turned around and walked beside her, saying nothing at all, which was oddly disquieting, so that she was glad when she reached the shop. He made no effort to go inside with her, and she sighed with relief as she closed the door on him. She was half-way through her shopping when Mr Drew said, 'What's he want, then? Hanging round outside… Why doesn't he come in instead of looking through the door like that?'

'I expect he's waiting for me.'

'Sweet on you, is he? Can't say I blame him.' And Mr Drew chuckled.

She spun out the order for as long as she could, but finally she had to leave the shop. Colin was strolling down the street some way from her and she crossed over and started on her way back home, to find him within seconds beside her again. There was no one about, so she stopped and faced him.

'Look, Colin, you're wasting your time. I have no intention of marrying you, and you would do better to find another job instead of hanging around here.'

He laughed. 'Come off it, darling. You were sweet on me and you can't deny it—led me on, you did, letting me think that your father would give me a partnership, or at least put up the money for us to settle down somewhere without money worries.'

'I did not lead you on.' Her voice rose indignantly, 'You're talking nonsense.'

He caught her by the arm and began walking down the street. 'We're going to have a talk, Beatrice, darling...'

She tried to pull away from him, but he was gripping her hard and just for a moment she felt scared; to make a scene wouldn't do at all... She closed her eyes for a moment, and when she opened them it was to see Oliver driving slowly up the street towards them. Her voice came out in a whisper and then a healthy shout, not that it had been necessary; she saw that he had seen them and was already pulling into the kerb, and a moment afterwards was standing before them, smiling a little.

'Oliver,' she was quite uncaring of the effect of her words, 'Oliver, do explain to Colin that we are engaged; I can't make him understand that I won't marry him.'

The doctor's smile didn't alter at all. 'My dear girl, until everyone reads of it in the *Telegraph*, no one knows.' He turned an almost benevolent face upon Colin. 'I dare say Beatrice had no chance to tell you, had she?'

He tucked a large hand under her arm, and she had never been so glad to feel its firm pressure. Colin looked from one to the other of them.

'Why didn't you tell me?' he demanded of Beatrice.

'You didn't give me the chance, but now you know, Colin, so please leave me alone.'

'I've been wasting my time,' he said furiously. 'Well, I wish you the best of luck, the pair of you.'

He turned on his heel and walked away, back up the street, and Beatrice watched him go in silence. Presently she said, 'I'm sorry—I panicked. And I had to stop him—I mean, right in the middle of the village, and you know how people look out of their windows—and he was holding me rather tightly—I didn't want to make a scene.'

The doctor listened patiently to this. 'You acted most sensibly,' he observed, at his most placid. 'And

I have no doubt that we shall shortly see the last of young Wood.'

He bent a thoughtful gaze upon her worried face. 'There's really nothing that he can do, you know.'

'No. But what about—that is, I said that we were engaged.'

'Very wise. I'll see that a notice goes into the *Telegraph* tomorrow morning.'

'But we're not.'

'Ah, you know that and I know that, but no one else needs to know. Tell your family by all means, but let everyone else believe what they read. Once Wood is safely away, we can review the situation.'

'Yes, but...'

'Shall we get into the car? I was on my way to see you—we will go the long way round and discuss the matter in comfort.'

So she got into the car beside him, aware now that several interested faces were peering round cottage curtains.

'We seem to have created a good deal of interest,' remarked the doctor calmly. He tooled the car gently up the street, turned past the pub and took a narrow lane just beyond it. 'Now, what is worrying you?'

'Us—you. You said you would put a notice in the *Telegraph*, but if you're going to get married, won't she mind? The girl you're going to marry?'

'She is a most sensible young woman; I foresee no difficulties. Besides, I intend to marry her and no one else. No one else really matters.'

He spoke quietly, and Beatrice felt a pang of envy for the girl who could be so sure of him whatever he did. He must love her very much. 'She must be awfully nice.'

'She is everything I could wish for. Do you intend to tell your mother?'

'Well, yes, I think so, but not Father, because then I'd have to explain about Colin and he might get upset and angry.' She thought for a bit. 'But I'd better tell Ella.'

The doctor laughed. 'A good idea—she's an observant child.'

'Were you coming to see Father?'

'Partly, and partly to see how you were getting on with Wood; I rather thought he would be a nuisance. Now you will be able to settle down to your usual quiet life again.'

Perversely, Beatrice found no pleasure in the prospect. She was thankful that Colin would be gone, but a quiet life, stretching ahead for years and years, held no appeal. There was always James, but she suspected that he had transferred his affections to the rector's eldest daughter, a friend of hers and most suitable for him. Without a tinge of regret, she hoped that they would be very happy.

'Perhaps it might be a good idea if you were to go away for a week or two. No need to say where you are going to anyone but your family. Colin—if he hasn't already gone—might possibly get the idea that you were staying with me, which might speed his departure.'

'Oh, does he know where you live?'

'No, but he knows that I work mostly in London; even if he wanted to find you, he might not find it worthwhile.'

'Why should he persist? I thought he would go away now.'

'It is to be hoped that he will, but you must remember that you are the key to everything he wants: a partnership, the prospect of taking over the practice in the future, and a wife who is by no means penniless.'

'And I thought it was just me,' she said ruefully.

Her father was over at the clinic, helping Mr Sharpe with an unexpectedly busy morning surgery; her mother was sitting outside the kitchen door, shelling peas.

'Your father won't be long now. Go and make the coffee, will you, darling? Oliver, can you spare the time to have a cup with us? You've come to see your patient, I expect?'

He sat down on the grass beside her, and when Beatrice had gone to the house she added, 'He's so much better now Colin has gone; he didn't like him, you know, and he was so afraid that Beatrice would fall in love with him.' She glanced sideways at the doctor's impassive face. 'I think she was beginning to, but now he's gone...' She heaved a sigh of relief.

'He hasn't gone, Mrs Browning. He's in the village, and he's been pestering Beatrice every time she pokes that pretty nose of hers outside this house.'

Mrs Browning stopped shelling peas and stared at him, open-mouthed. 'Pestering her? She has never said a word.'

'She doesn't want to upset Mr Browning. It was quite by chance that I found out about it.'

'And?'

Beatrice came through the door with the tray, and he got up and took it from her. 'I think Beatrice may want to tell you herself.'

'But not her father?' Mrs Browning began to pour the coffee. 'He'll be another ten minutes or so, dear. Oliver has just told me that Colin has been bothering you—has he gone or do we send you away? Is it upsetting you?' She handed the doctor a mug of coffee and then a plate of biscuits. 'Of course, you don't have to say anything if you don't feel like it.'

'Well, Mother—' began Beatrice, and gave her an admirably brief account of Colin's activities. 'And then this morning I couldn't get rid of him and—and I saw Oliver and I shouted to him, and he came and I told Colin that we were engaged...' She heard her mother's sharp intake of breath. 'Yes, I know, I must have been a little mad, but I couldn't think of anything else, and Oliver very kindly told a lot of fibs about the notice being in the *Telegraph* tomorrow...'

She hadn't looked at Oliver once as she talked, but now she looked across at him. 'I am very grateful, I really am, and I hope you didn't think I was imposing on your good nature.'

'Think nothing of it.' His voice was nicely casual. 'I have hopes that your quick thinking may have the right effect. All the same, I think that you should go away for a week or so; it will save answering awkward questions in the village, and give Wood no opportunity of cross-questioning you. Another thing, perhaps it might be a good idea to mention our engagement to your father. There is no need to say anything about Wood, and we can be vague about the future. After a suitable interval, Beatrice, you can change your mind and we can all go back to our normal way of living.'

A sensible speech which left both Beatrice and her mother with feelings of regret, but for different reasons.

'And what about you, Oliver?' asked Mrs Browning worriedly. 'Won't it interfere with your life— your private life?'

'I don't believe so. I'm going on a lecture tour in a few days' time, so I shall see very few of my friends for several weeks, and I shall have a backlog of work to get through on my return, so I'm not likely to go out a great deal.'

'You make it sound very easy.'

He passed his mug for more coffee. 'My tour takes in Utrecht, Cologne, Copenhagen, Brussels and finally Edinburgh; it will take a fortnight, or perhaps a day or two more than that. In fact, I can see no reason why Beatrice shouldn't come with me. Lecturers usually take wives with them, and it is by no means unusual for fiancées to go along.' He had spoken in his usual calm fashion; now he looked at Beatrice and smiled. 'A good idea? No hurry to decide. I shall be at Salisbury for the next day or so. I'll give you a ring before I go back.'

He got to his feet as Mr Browning joined them, remarking that he looked fit and well. 'I'll take a look if I may before I go, although I'm sure that I shall find everything satisfactory.'

Mr Browning sat down. 'You all look very pleased with yourselves,' he observed.

It was Beatrice who answered. 'Father, Oliver and I—we've got engaged. It was rather sudden and we haven't any plans at present; Oliver's busy.'

'My dear, what splendid news! Oliver, I am delighted. And here have I been worrying about young Wood. I quite thought that you were beginning to like him, Beatrice, and all the time it was Oliver. Well, well!' He beamed around him. 'Now I shall have to find someone to take your place.'

'Not yet, Father,' said Beatrice quickly. 'Oliver has an awful lot of work to get through.' And, when he looked doubtful, she added hastily, 'You know who is longing to step into my shoes? Ella—she might even train as a vet. She's been pestering me to let her work at the clinic during her holidays, and they begin next week.'

She succeeded in her efforts to divert his thoughts.

'You're quite right, Beatrice—she is a natural with animals. There's no reason why she shouldn't help out with exercising and feeding and learning something of the surgical work.' He put down his mug. 'I dare say you're busy, Oliver. Shall we go indoors? I never felt better in my life, especially now that I've heard your news. Beatrice will make a splendid wife, you know—a very level-headed girl and an excellent cook.'

He led the way indoors and Beatrice said softly, 'Oh, Mother, I don't think it will work—what have I started?'

Her mother gave her an untroubled look. 'Well, darling, it struck me that Oliver didn't seem all that surprised—I mean, one would have thought that he had thought of it himself.'

There was the faintest question in her remark.

'As a matter of fact,' said Beatrice carefully, 'he did—not then, but before Colin left he was being tiresome one morning—' Somehow she couldn't bring herself to tell her mother about Colin's telephone conversation which she had overheard. 'And Oliver happened to come along, and we had a talk afterwards and he suggested that it might be an idea, but I said no.'

'Things have a way of sorting themselves out,' observed Mrs Browning. She sounded quite pleased.

The two men came back presently, and after a few minutes' reassuring talk from the doctor he drove

away with nothing more than a casual remark to Beatrice that he would see her in a day or two.

True to his word, the announcement of their engagement appeared in the *Telegraph* on the following
day, and Beatrice spent the day answering phone
calls from friends and people she knew in the village.
There was a phone call from Great-Aunt Sybil too,
with guarded approval of the match. 'A well-
mannered young man,' she observed weightily, 'and
Miss Moore, whom he recommended to me, has
proved to be a treasure. He is one of the few mem-
bers of the medical profession who has an inkling of
my needs.'

A recommendation which Beatrice stored away to
pass on to Oliver when next she saw him.

There was a letter from Colin the following morning, and she saw with misgiving that she was right
in thinking he was still in the village. It was an impassioned missive, and if she hadn't had the clear
memory of his phone conversation she might have
been swayed by it. She read it carefully, tore it up
and put the pieces tidily in the wastepaper basket. If
she ignored it, he would surely go.

Only he didn't; he was still there three days later,
sending her a letter each day, not attempting to see
her, only begging her to break off her engagement
and marry him instead. 'Your father won't object,'
he had written, 'once he realises it is what you want;
he can offer me a partnership and we can have
Sharpe's house.' Only someone as selfish as he could

suggest turning a man and his family out of house and job, thought Beatrice, and tore up yet another letter.

The doctor came on the evening of the fourth day, quiet and self-assured, and when she had poured out all her worries he remarked placidly, 'We can take care of that; you'll come on the tour with me. I'll have Miss Cross with me, so you won't lack for company while I'm lecturing. I'm leaving the day after tomorrow. Can you be ready by then? You have a passport? Good. Bring clothes for a couple of weeks, and something to wear at the rather boring dinner parties we shall attend.'

He smiled at her rather in the manner of a medical man who had just reassured his patient that she would get better, even if she didn't think so at that moment.

'Are you sure? I mean, won't your fiancée mind?'

He said evenly, 'The girl I am going to marry will have no objection.'

'Then she must be a saint,' said Beatrice roundly.

'Happily, no. Just flesh and blood, nicely put together.'

'Do you want me to come up to London?'

'No. I'll fetch you some time in the morning, and I shall drive very slowly down the village street so that everyone will be able to see us go.'

'You think of everything.'

'I do my best.' He sounded amused.

'But what about when we get back?'

'Let us cross our bridges when we get to them. The whole point of the exercise is to convince Wood that you are really unattainable. Let us deal with that first. What have you done with his letters?'

'Torn them up. At least, one came this morning, but I haven't read it yet.'

'Then do so while I take a look at your father. His surgery will be over by now?'

'Yes.' He had stopped the car short of the house, and she had been the only one to see him drive up. 'I'll go and make the coffee. I'll be in the kitchen.'

Her mother was there, stringing beans while Mrs Perry cleaned the kitchen. She had been with the family for too long for anyone to have qualms about minding their 'p's and 'q's in front of her.

'Oliver's here,' said Beatrice. 'He's gone to see Father—he's staying for coffee. He wants me to go on his lecture tour with him and his secretary the day after tomorrow.'

'Now won't that be a treat?' remarked Mrs Perry. 'All over the place, no doubt, and plenty of fine folk to listen to him.'

'Well, yes, I suppose so. My passport's all right for another year—it's ten years, isn't it? And I had it for that trip after I took my A levels.'

'Clothes?' enquired her mother, getting to the heart of the matter. 'Will you go anywhere?' She meant, would Beatrice go anywhere special where she would need to dress up?

'Well, dinners and things. It's for about a fort-night.'

'Make the coffee, darling, will you? Ella's home, luckily. You and I will go to Bath this afternoon and do some shopping. What's that letter in your hand?'

Beatrice had forgotten Colin's letter. She opened it while the coffee brewed and read it slowly. It was even more urgent than the others—he couldn't un-derstand why she hadn't answered his letters; surely she must see what a splendid future they could have together? Once again he pointed out that her father was bound to see them on their feet and make sure that she continued to live comfortably as she had always done.

'Well, really,' declared Beatrice indignantly, just as the doctor came into the kitchen; he removed the letter from her hand and read it.

He tore it into pieces when he had done so, and put them into the kitchen bin, and said placidly, 'Your father is remarkably fit—not to be worried, of course. Mr Sharpe seems to be just right for him—they get on well together.' He took the tray from Beatrice. 'In the garden?'

'I'll have mine here, young man,' declared Mrs Perry, and remembered a bit late to add, 'Doctor.'

Mrs Browning sliced the last bean. She was dying of curiosity to know what had been in the letter, but four daughters had taught her the value of a golden silence. This time, however, she was to have her re-ward.

With a glance at Beatrice, the doctor said casually, 'His letters don't vary, do they? The promise of a vague future, but no mention of how that will be achieved. A dish of herbs where love is is all very well, but nowadays one needs the money to buy the herbs.'

Mrs Browning chuckled. 'Poor boy; I still don't like him—but I'm a little sorry for him, too.'

Beatrice said nothing, but busied herself with the coffee, and the doctor said smoothly, 'From all accounts he is a good vet; he should be able to get a job wherever he wants to go.'

He accepted a mug of coffee and Beatrice gave him a grateful look; her mother was satisfied about the contents of the letter; he had somehow managed to dispel any suspicions she might have had about Colin, and at the same time implied that he would recover quickly enough from his professed love of Beatrice.

When her father joined them, the doctor asked in his mildest manner, 'You will be coming with me, Beatrice?' He glanced across at Mr Browning, who nodded happily. 'I've rushed you, rather, but I'm sure you will enjoy yourself. I don't have much time during the day, but Miss Cross is a pleasant companion. I'll be taking the car and we'll go from Dover and drive up from Calais. We shall be in Utrecht for two days.'

He glanced at Beatrice. 'Come back to my place

for lunch, Beatrice, and I'll tell you exactly where we are going.'

She shook her head. 'I'd have liked to, but Mother and I are going to Bath—I must do some shopping...'

'Ah, of course, you will have nothing to wear.' His voice was bland. 'In that case, come to lunch, then we'll pick Mrs Browning up and I'll drive you both there and collect you whenever you say.' He added with a faint smile, 'I have some shopping to do, too.'

No one could find fault with this; Beatrice went indoors to change her dress and find Ella to beg her to take Knotty for his walk, then hurried outside again. They were still sitting over their coffee, but Oliver got up when he saw her, said his goodbyes and ushered her into the car in a businesslike manner, and drove off.

CHAPTER SIX

THE DOCTOR had little to say as he drove to his home, and Beatrice, her head for the moment full of worried thoughts about her clothes, hardly noticed his silence. She had nice clothes; her father paid her a salary for her help at the clinic and she was able to afford them, but she didn't go out a great deal and her stock of after-six dresses was small. 'And something to travel in,' she muttered, forgetting where she was for the moment.

'Oh, knitted cotton or jersey that will drip dry,' Oliver answered.

She turned to gape at him. 'Whatever do you know about drip-dry cotton?'

'You forget that I have sisters. You should wear honey colour with that hair, or that pale apricot pink. I'm partial to pink.'

She had to laugh, and he said, 'That's better. You don't laugh enough these days.'

He swept the car through the gates, and there was Jennings waiting at the open door with Mabel bouncing around, anxious to be made much of. Beatrice, going in to a chorus of cheerful barks and Jennings hovering, felt quite at home.

They ate their lunch with a map spread out on the

128

table between them, while the doctor pointed out exactly where they would be going.

'And do you lecture in English?' she wanted to know.

'In Holland, yes, and in Copenhagen, but I manage to make myself understood in German and French, and of course a number of medical terms are universal.'

'And do you give the same lecture each time?'

'Well, basically, yes.'

'You must be very clever—cleverer than I thought…'

He said gravely, 'Thank you, Beatrice. You flatter me.'

'Oh, I didn't mean to do that,' she said forthrightly. 'I dare say there are a lot of things you can't do.'

His, 'Oh, dozens,' was so meek that she gave him a suspicious look which he countered with a bland smile.

They didn't linger over the meal, but got back into the car, this time with Mabel on the back seat, and drove back to her home. Mrs Browning, hatted and gloved, was waiting for them, declared herself perfectly willing to share the back seat with Mabel and was ushered into the car.

The journey took less than an hour, and was largely filled by Mrs Browning's voice murmuring over her shopping list.

'You'll need a new dress, dear; something pretty for the evening...'

Beatrice frowned; it sounded as though her mother was fishing for dinner invitations; if he offered her one she would refuse.

The doctor caught the frown out of the corner of his eye and smiled a little. 'Two, if I might suggest that. I did tell Beatrice that I am invited to attend at least one dinner in each place we visit, and I'm expected to bring my companion.'

'What about Miss Cross?' Beatrice asked.

'Oh, the secretaries have a gathering of their own; she has what she calls her little black number, and something called her brown crêpe.'

'You look awful in black,' commented Mrs Browning from the back seat.

Beatrice let out a very small sigh, and the doctor began to talk about the journey, so that Mrs Browning put away her list and listened. He could, on occasion, talk 'nothings' with great charm.

He dropped them off at the top of Milsom Street, promised to pick them up at the same place at half-past five, and drove away with Mabel sitting beside him.

Mrs Browning gave a satisfied sigh. 'Now, let me see—Brown's first, I think, darling. Your father told me that you had to have all that you needed. You buy what you want; I've my cheque-book with me.'

'Mother, I have plenty of money—I've not spent anything for weeks.'

'Yes, dear, but your father would like to give you a present—you've been so good and helpful.'

The two of them plunged into a delightful afternoon's shopping, emerging after an hour or so with a great many parcels and a much thinner chequebook. Beatrice had found the knitted three-piece almost at once. What was more, it was in an apricot pink. 'Quite uncrushable,' declared the saleslady, 'and so suitable.' She didn't say what it was suitable for, but that hardly mattered; Beatrice was well satisfied. She had found two pretty dresses too—just in case she needed them, she pointed out to her mother. 'And since Father's paying...'

A patterned crêpe, very elegant with long, tight sleeves and a billowing skirt, and a blouse and skirt in satin, the blouse ivory, the skirt in a rich, dark red. To these were added a cotton dress with its matching cardigan, and a sun dress she thought she might never have the chance to wear, but which suited her so well that it seemed a pity not to buy it. They had tea at a nice teashop, and punctually at half-past five returned to the spot where Oliver was to meet them. He was already there, reading an evening paper, one arm round Mabel. No one, thought Beatrice, looking at him, would guess that he was an eminent physician at the very top of his profession. He looked far too much at ease. He looked up and, aware of them, got out of the car, ushered Mabel into the back, disposed of their parcels, tucked Mrs Browning smoothly in beside Mabel, whisked Beatrice into the front seat, climbed in beside her and drove off.

'I'm sorry we are a little late,' observed Beatrice.

'Five—ten minutes? I hadn't even glanced at my watch. Did you have a successful afternoon?'

'Oh, very, thank you. Did you?'

'I? Oh, yes. A consultation at Bath United.'

'Oh, do they call you in there as well?'

His firm mouth twitched with a hidden smile. 'I get called in all over the place.'

'Well, yes, I suppose you do.' They were silent while she tried to think of something to say, and couldn't. Her mother broke the long silence.

'You'll stay for supper, Oliver? Nothing much, just one of my pork pies with a salad and duchesse potatoes. Beatrice made a strawberry tart this morning—with cream, of course.'

'I'm going back to London this evening, Mrs Browning; I've a round to do in the morning and patients to see...'

'Well, you have to eat and it will be quite ready; I warned Ella. She's almost as good a cook as Beatrice.'

'In that case, I'll stay with the greatest of pleasure. You don't object to Mabel?'

'Good heavens, no! She can have her supper with Knotty. I dare say she'll be glad of a run around the garden. Will she go back with you this evening?'

'Oh, yes. She hates London, but she hates being away from me more.'

They talked about dogs for the rest of the journey.

Supper was a lively meal; no one mentioned Colin, the talk was all of Mr Browning's day at the clinic, the afternoon's shopping and the forthcoming trip.

Oliver could have known us all his life, thought Beatrice, watching him gently teasing Ella and carrying the dishes out to the kitchen. She thought it unlikely that the Jenningses allowed him to tidy away so much as a fork. He said all the right things to Mr and Mrs Browning, received a kiss from Ella with every sign of pleasure, waved casually to Beatrice, begged her to be ready when he came for her on the following day and drove away.

She went away to pack her bag, make sure that she had her passport and money while she listened to Ella's good advice about the right make-up and how to do her hair. 'You can't go around with a plait,' she pointed out. 'Do a french pleat or a chignon, and do use eye-shadow.' She sighed. 'I wish I had your eyelashes...'

To all of which Beatrice listened with only half an ear; she was thinking about Colin, although her thoughts were strangely clouded by a strong mental picture of the doctor. At least, she thought, by the time she got back home Colin would have gone and she would be able to stop thinking about him. She hated him for his duplicity, but at the same time it was hard to shake off the attraction she had felt for him.

'Don't look so sad,' said Ella. 'You're not old yet.

You never know, you may meet a dashing Dutchman or a German professor.'

'I don't fancy either.' Beatrice began to loop her hair into a tidy chignon. 'Besides, I don't expect to meet any.'

'You're going to those dinner parties Oliver hates; find him a sexy blonde and hunt around for yourself.'

Beatrice let her hair fall round her shoulders. 'Ella, where do you get your ideas from? You're only fifteen…'

'Darling Beatrice, you're the one who's fifteen—being taken in by Colin like a teenager and not having an idea how to deal with him. You're a darling, but you've spent too many years with animals and not enough with men.'

To which remark Beatrice agreed, being an honest girl.

Wearing the new jersey outfit, she was ready when Oliver arrived.

His greeting was decidedly casual. 'Ah—you took my advice.' His eyes swept over her person; the casual look of a brother for a sister, she reflected peevishly. 'You're ready? We must go up to town and pick up Miss Cross. I told her to be at the flat—we can have lunch there and then drive down to Dover.'

They drove to town, making small talk in a desultory fashion, eating up the miles until the outskirts of London slowed them down. Beatrice had only the vaguest idea where the doctor lived; she supposed that it was somewhere close to his consulting-rooms in Harley Street—perhaps he lived in a flat at the same house.

He didn't. He drove up Park Lane, turned off into South Audley Street and, just short of Grosvenor Square, entered a quiet little tree-lined street with a terrace of Regency houses on either side. Almost at its end, he drew up.

'Oh, is this where you live?'

'When I'm in London, yes. Come along, we haven't a great deal of time.'

She was bustled across the narrow pavement to the front door, opened as they reached it by a tall, thin woman with a severe expression, made even more severe by the way her hair was drawn back into a tight bun and her lack of make-up.

'Hello, Rosie,' said the doctor cheerfully. 'I hope you've got a good lunch for us. Is Miss Cross here?'

'Good day to you, Doctor.' The faintest glimmer of a smile did its best. 'Lunch will be served in ten minutes, and Miss Cross arrived not five minutes ago.'

'Splendid. This is Miss Browning. Beatrice, Rosie runs my home for me and is indispensable.'

Beatrice shook hands and murmured and Rosie said graciously, 'If Miss Browning will come with me, I'll show her where she may tidy herself.'

Beatrice wasn't aware that she was untidy, but she went meekly enough in the wake of Rosie to the end of the narrow, elegant hall where there was a splendidly appointed cloakroom. Presently, hoping that

she would fulfil Rosie's expectations of tidiness, she
went back into the hall.

The doctor poked his head out of a door as she
did so. 'In here, Beatrice,' he said, and drew her into
a charming room overlooking the street, furnished
with deep armchairs and sofas and several very nice
Regency tables bearing reading-lamps. Cosy in the
winter, thought Beatrice, and advanced to meet Miss
Cross.

She had imagined her to be a smart, youngish
woman, exquisitely made-up, dressed with fashionable elegance and full of the social graces. Miss
Cross was none of these things; she was dumpy and
little and well into her forties, with a round face and
twinkly eyes and a neat head of brown hair, going
unashamedly grey. She was dressed neatly but un-
fashionably, and on the front of her dress hung her
gold-rimmed spectacles. Beatrice liked her at once,
and they beamed at each other as the doctor introduced them. 'Here's Beatrice, Ethel. Beatrice, Ethel
has been with me for a long time now; she always
knows where I have to go next and what I have to
do—I'd be lost without her.'

'Such nonsense,' declared Ethel delightedly. 'How
nice to meet you—may I call you Beatrice?'

'Oh, please—and may I call you Ethel?'

'Let us drink to that,' observed the doctor, handing
round sherry.

They lunched in a smaller room at the back of the
house, furnished in mahogany and with french win-

dows opening on to a charming little garden. There was a bird-bath at the end of the centre path, and sitting on a bench near the window was a large tortoiseshell cat, watching two kittens playing on the small lawn.

'Rosie's pet,' observed Oliver, settling Beatrice in her chair. 'Her name's Popsie. She joined the household some months ago and took over the kitchen regions, and I suspect that the kittens have every intention of taking up residence with her. Rosie adores cats.'

'Does Mabel mind when she comes here?'

'Not in the least. But she doesn't like London, although she comes up and down with me.'

Rosie served lunch: lettuce soup, grilled sole and a salad, and a fresh fruit salad for afters. The coffee was delicious and served with tiny butter biscuits made, Oliver assured her, by Rosie to a secret recipe.

He was so well served, she reflected; Rosie here, obviously devoted to him despite her severity, and the Jenningses at his home in Dorset. But he deserved it, she conceded; his was a relentless life, despite the comfort of his living, and he wasn't a man who, having reached the top, would seek an easy life.

They didn't linger over the meal; Miss Cross was ushered into the back seat of the car, Beatrice got into the seat beside the doctor, and they began their journey.

They went over on the hovercraft and, since Ethel Cross and Oliver were both immersed in papers,

Beatrice opened the paperback she had had the fore-
thought to bring with her, and pretended to read. The
doctor raised his eyes once to say, 'Sorry we're so
unsociable, but it's an opportunity to get everything
sorted out. My first lecture is tomorrow morning at
nine o'clock, and we have to have some kind of plan
for the day. Ethel will be with me, taking notes, but
we'll meet you for lunch. I'll tell you where.'

On land, he drove steadily, stopping for tea just
before they crossed the Dutch border. Miss Cross had
dozed for most of the journey, and he and Beatrice
had carried on a conversation which needed very little effort on either's part.

The doctor had taken the motorway through An-
twerp and Breda, and entered Utrecht from the south.
As they neared the city centre, Beatrice stared round
her as he threaded his way through the evening traffic, pointing out the cathedral tower and the cathedral, the canals and the brief glimpse of the fish mar-
ket. 'There's plenty to see,' he told her, 'and no
difficulty with the language. I'm afraid Ethel and I
will have to leave you to your own devices until the
late afternoon, but we'll go out in the evening.'

She had expected that. 'I'll be quite all right,' she
assured him. 'I like pottering.' And indeed, the city
looked worth exploring, with its old houses and tree-
lined canals. She wondered where they were to stay,
and got her answer almost at once when he stopped
before a hotel in the heart of the city. It looked grand

in an old-fashioned way, and just for a moment she had qualms, to be reassured by Ethel's friendly voice.

'This is most comfortable. We stayed here a year ago when the doctor came over to test the medical students and deliver a lecture. And everyone speaks English.'

They had rooms on the first floor, Beatrice and Ethel beside each other and the doctor on the opposite side of the corridor. The rooms were extremely comfortable, with large bathrooms and balconies overlooking the street, and Ethel's had a table in the window on which she put her portable typewriter. 'We'll have breakfast together,' she told Beatrice cheerfully, 'and probably lunch, but I have dinner when it suits me; I like to get my notes written up each evening.'

Beatrice didn't like to ask about Oliver's arrangements; she supposed that he would meet colleagues in the evenings, so probably she would dine with Ethel. She went to her own room to unpack, mindful of the doctor's suggestion that they should all meet in the bar in an hour's time.

Bathed, her hair hanging down her back, she began to worry about what she should wear. She dragged on her dressing-gown and nipped out into the corridor. There was no one about, so she put the door latch up and started the few yards along the corridor to Ethel's door. She had her hand raised to knock when a small sound behind her sent her whizzing round. Oliver was standing at his open door, watching her.

'Oh, hello. I'm just going to ask Ethel what to wear…'

'You look very nice like that. I like the hair.' He watched with interest while she blushed. 'Wear whatever women wear to cocktail parties. I'm not a betting man, but I'm willing to wager a substantial sum on the certainty of Ethel's wearing her little black number.'

Beatrice edged her way back to her own door. 'Oh, well, thank you…'

He hadn't moved. He glanced at his watch now. 'You have fifteen minutes.'

She sat down at her dressing-table and did her rather flushed face and wound her hair into a smooth chignon, then got into the patterned crêpe, found slippers and evening bag, and with barely a minute to spare tapped on Ethel's door.

The doctor's money had been quite safe; Miss Cross was wearing the little black number, a sober dress with a discreet neckline and all the same elegant enough. She eyed Beatrice appreciatively.

'That's pretty,' she exclaimed. 'And of course, you have a lovely figure, if I may say so. I'd love to be able to wear a dress like that; it's a lovely fit.'

They went down together, talking clothes, and the doctor watched them coming down the staircase and across the foyer. He sighed gently and went to meet them.

Dinner was delightful, and the three of them were in the best of good spirits, but after Miss Cross had had one cup of coffee she declared that she would go to her room and get things ready for the morning.

'That first lecture, Doctor,' she wanted to know, 'you will be finished by eleven o'clock, I take it? Then you'll have coffee and see some cases at the St Antonius Ziekenhuis. Where will you lunch, and will you need me there?'

'No, Ethel, you're free until half-past one, when I'm due at the Whilhelmina Kinderziekenhuis. I'll want you there, but I don't expect to stay after five o'clock.' He stood up as she got to her feet. 'Don't worry about Beatrice, I'll see about her lunch, and don't forget there's a dinner in the evening.'

She beamed at them both. 'You'll enjoy that. I'll see you at breakfast.'

He sat down again and ordered more coffee. 'Now, let us get your day settled...'

'You don't have to bother about me. I shall be perfectly all right all day.'

She might just as well not have spoken. 'Will you come to the St Antonius Ziekenhuis at twelve-fifteen? Take a taxi. It's quite a short ride. We'll have lunch at the Hotel des Pays Bas in the bar there; the children's hospital is very central. You'll come to dinner at the university in the evening—half-past eight. The next day I have to lecture at the Academisch Ziekenhuis, that's very central; then there will

be a noonday reception there—you'll come to that.
We leave in the afternoon.'

She eyed him askance. He had it all nicely
planned, and she wondered what he would say if she
declined to join in his plans. On the other hand, he
had been kind enough to help her out of the awkward
situation with Colin. 'Very well, I'll do as you ask.
Thank you for your kind invitations,' she added politely.

He gave a rumble of laughter. 'Am I walking
roughshod over your plans? I'm sorry if I'm bustling
you around. I only wish I had more time to show
you round, but you have no need to get lost, I'll get
a city plan for you from the desk and you can always
ask, you're a sensible girl.'

She busied herself with the coffee-cups. She had
taken pains with her appearance that evening, and all
he could say was that she was sensible. A pity she
hadn't bought a little black number like Ethel's.

'You're looking peevish,' said Oliver, putting his
finger unerringly on the spot. 'I called you sensible,
and I've not once said how charming you look this
evening, and if I say it now it won't do at all, will
it?'

She said thoughtfully, 'Well, I suppose that it
would be better than nothing,' and he laughed again.

'Would you like to go somewhere and dance?'

She was too surprised to answer at once. 'Dance?
Us? Isn't it rather late?'

'Very relaxing after a long drive. There's a place

close by—we can walk there.' He smiled with such charm that she found herself smiling back at him. 'You'll need a shawl or something.'

She had a mohair stole with her; she went to her room and fetched it, and went back to the foyer where he was waiting for her. If they danced for an hour it would still be not quite midnight by the time she got to bed, and perhaps he needed to unwind. He didn't look as though he needed to unwind, she reflected as she went to meet him, and for a fleeting moment thought of Colin, who would have rushed to meet her as though she were the only girl in the world. She gave her head a little shake; she mustn't think of him any more. She had come away in order to forget him, and there was nothing wrong with the doctor's manners; they were, in fact, a good deal better than Colin's. Without haste he had reached her side, wrapped her stole around her shoulders and accompanied her to the door where he took her arm. 'Less than five minutes' walk,' he told her, 'and it's a lovely night.'

The club overlooked a canal; discreetly quiet and just full enough to make it pleasant and a little exciting. They had a table near the dance-floor and the doctor ordered champagne. In the becoming light of pink-shaded lamps Beatrice drank a glass and got up willingly enough to dance. She danced well, but then so did Oliver and the band was good. It was two hours later when she asked him the time and declared roundly that they should both be in bed. 'You've a lecture at nine o'clock,' she reminded him, 'and you've been driving all day. If you don't get some sleep, you'll forget what you have to say.'

'Oh, Ethel would never allow that; she hands me a sheaf of typed notes at the very last minute.' He spoke seriously, although she had the strong impression that he was laughing at her.

'So that you can read them—what a good idea.'

'Isn't it? I haven't done so so far, but I hold them in my hand or put them on the table before me so as not to hurt her feelings.'

They walked back to the hotel and said goodnight in the foyer. 'I enjoyed dancing,' said Beatrice. 'I do hope that you are not too tired.'

He smiled down at her, and for no reason at all she had the feeling that she had said something foolish. 'Never too tired to dance with you, Beatrice. Goodnight and sleep well.'

She contrived to peep over her shoulder as she reached the head of the staircase; he was still standing at its foot, watching her.

As she got ready for bed she told herself that he was a man of the world, well-versed in the art of flattering a woman. On the other hand, she mused, she had to admit he had been kind to her; and not just kind, he had offered practical help when she had needed it most, as well as a shoulder as solid as a rock upon which she had cried her eyes out. Her last thought as she drifted off into sleep was that he was a very nice man. Nice was a useful adjective—it cov-

ered a dozen others more specific, but she was too
sleepy to think of them.

Breakfast was a businesslike meal with the doctor
and Ethel arranging the day between them, although
as they rose from the table he reiterated his plans for
Beatrice, adding, 'Have you sufficient money with
you?'

She had a small bundle of traveller's cheques in
her bag. 'Oh, more than enough.'

They walked through the foyer together, and she
stood with him while Ethel went to her room to get
her coat and notebook. 'I hope you have a successful
lecture. I hope you'll let me come and listen to
one...'

He lifted his eyebrows. 'Why, thank you, Beatrice,
and so you shall.' There was no time to say any
more, for Ethel had joined them.

'There are some lovely shops,' she told Beatrice,
and started for the door.

'Don't spend all your money,' begged the doctor,
then bent and kissed Beatrice's surprised mouth, and
had gone before she could do more than gasp.

She left the hotel half an hour later, and spent the
morning window-shopping and buying one or two
presents to take home; she sent a postcard too, had
coffee at a chic little coffee-shop and went to gaze
at the cathedral. She would have liked to have spent
longer; she would have to go back a second time,
there was so much to see, and she wanted to walk
through the cloisters before it was time to get her

taxi. There were quite a few people around, but the cloisters were peaceful all the same. She wandered around and found herself wishing that Oliver was with her, and although she thought of Colin, too, she had to admit that the doctor would be a far better companion in such surroundings. She sighed for no reason and went to look for a taxi.

It was exactly a quarter-past twelve as she paid off the taxi and went through the hospital entrance, uncertain what she should do if Oliver were not there. But he was, talking to two other older men and when he saw her he went to meet her, took her arm and introduced them to her. She shook hands and answered their polite questions, which were uttered in pedantic English, and when Oliver said they should be going they expressed the hope that they would see her that evening. The older of them twinkled nicely at her, and added, 'I do not see why our good friend here should have you all to himself!'

Oliver smiled and said nothing, and Beatrice murmured politely, registering a vow that, given the chance, she would take good care that he saw as little as possible of her at the dinner. She could of course plead a headache and cry off, but on second thoughts that would be a mean thing to do. In his own fashion, Oliver had helped her a lot, even though at times she had found herself thinking that it was more from a sense of duty than actual friendship.

She accompanied him to the car presently, talking pleasantly about her morning and making all the proper enquiries as to his lecture. They were seated at a small window table, studying the menu, when he observed blandly, 'What a little chatterbox you are, Beatrice—you don't have to entertain me with small talk unless you feel that you must.'

Which left her speechless.

They ate in silence for some time, amused on the part of the doctor, peeved on her part, until he said mildly, 'I couldn't think of anything to say.' A remark which she didn't pretend not to understand. She laughed then. 'Never tell me that you were at a loss for words.'

'Certainly not, but I'm not sure if they would have been the right ones! Would you like coffee?'

The hatchet, a very small one, was buried; they spent the rest of the meal talking about Utrecht, and presently parted company. 'But mind you're back at the hotel by half-past four,' he reminded her. 'We can all have tea together and Ethel can remind me of what I have to do next.'

Beatrice spent the afternoon in the cathedral again; there were a great many other places to visit, but she knew that once she poked her nose into a museum she would lose all count of time. Obedient to Oliver's instructions, she presented herself in the hotel lounge exactly on time, and found him and Ethel already there. Over tea and delicious little biscuits they discussed their day, and when Ethel left them in order to type up her notes they stayed where they were, not saying much, pleased with each other's company.

It would have to be the long red satin skirt and the white blouse, decided Beatrice as she changed for the evening. And they really looked very glamorous and worth every penny of her father's money. She did her face and hair with extra care, thrust her feet into black satin evening pumps, found her matching bag and went downstairs. It was a fine, warm evening, so that the question of a coat or stole didn't arise. They would have spoilt the magic of the blouse and skirt most dreadfully.

She swanned down the rather grand hotel staircase, pleased with her appearance, and was rewarded by the look on Oliver's face when he saw her, although his rather casual, 'Oh, very nice,' was hardly flattering. The thought crossed her mind that probably she wasn't the type of girl he admired. This girl he was going to marry was very likely small and fair and blue-eyed and delightfully helpless. It was a pity, she reflected, accompanying him out to the car, that she was a big girl who, if ever she should faint, and that was most unlikely, would undoubtedly knock flat anyone she fell on to. She sat beside him, her self-confidence oozing through the soles of the pretty slippers she wore. And at the University, ushered relentlessly forward by her companion, she had a great desire to turn tail and run. There were many people milling round, the women all splendidly dressed. She felt Oliver's hand under her arm as she stood still, wishing very much that she wasn't there.

The doctor bent his head and whispered in her ear,

'You are easily the most beautiful woman here, Beatrice. Lift your chin and throw your shoulders back, and do me proud.'

She was so surprised that for the moment she didn't do anything at all, and when she looked up at him he was smiling, his face calm. She found herself smiling back, and all at once her peevishness melted away and she sailed along beside him to where the reception committee waited.

After that, the evening was a thundering success; she met any number of Oliver's colleagues and their wives, and managed very nicely on her own when he was compelled to leave her once or twice. She had him for a dinner partner though, with a stout, middle-aged man on her left, whose English was fluent, if heavily accented, and who paid her lavish compliments which she accepted with a pretty dignity and stored away to be recounted to Ella when she got home.

And after dinner people stood about talking, discussing future seminars and conferences while the women listened dutifully and managed to gossip among themselves at the same time. Beatrice, who was accepted, had she but known it, as Oliver's future wife, was led from group to group and made much of with frequent invitations to visit her new friends when she next came to Utrecht. To all of which she replied with a vagueness taken for shyness on her part.

It was late as they drove back to the hotel, and

there were very few people in the foyer. They left
the doorman to take the car to the garage, and wandered across the carpeted floor towards the staircase.

'Thank you for a lovely evening,' said Beatrice,
suddenly shy.

The doctor took her hand and turned her round to
face him. 'You enjoyed yourself? Good.' He sounded
remote. 'A change of scene is the best cure for a
damaged heart. It seems to be working well.'

She hadn't expected him to say anything like that.
It was as if he were reminding her that she was there
as one of his patients, being treated under his expert
eye. She suddenly wanted to cry without knowing
why, but she swallowed back the tears and said very
politely, 'I'm sure you're right. Goodnight.' And she
walked, with a very straight back, upstairs.

CHAPTER SEVEN

BEATRICE didn't sleep well; she was healthily tired, but she wasn't happy. She supposed that she was missing Colin, although she had the greatest difficulty conjuring up his face, even though she was able to remember very clearly the flattering remarks he had made so often. They hadn't meant anything, though.

It was going to be a warm day, so she put on a cotton dress and went down to breakfast. The doctor and Ethel were already at their table, but he got up as she joined them, and she sat down, soothed by his good manners. His good morning was brisk.

'Don't forget there's a farewell reception at noon at the Academisch Ziekenhuis. We will come back here for lunch and leave for Cologne in the afternoon. Ethel, you'll be there, of course. Beatrice, walk in to the hospital and say you're my guest; Ethel will come for you if I can't manage it. It will last about an hour, and you'll have met quite a few of the people there already.'

He had barely glanced at her, but Ethel had noted her tired face and, being the soul of discretion, had said nothing. Beatrice, unaware that his quick look had taken in her unhappy face, thanked him politely

and poured her coffee, buttered a croissant and took
a bite. She was feeling better already; the doctor's
bracing manner didn't allow time for melancholy,
and listening to Ethel's cheerful voice she felt
ashamed of her self-pity. They left the breakfast-table
presently and went their various ways with last-
minute instructions from the doctor as to the quickest
way to reach the Academisch Ziekenhuis from the
shopping centre.

The morning went pleasantly. She bought another
present or two, had coffee and then began to stroll
towards the hospital. She had gone to her room after
breakfast and changed into the pink jersey outfit; the
cotton dress hadn't seemed quite suitable for a reception, although the doctor hadn't said anything,
and she had done her face after she had had her coffee. The doctor, watching her cross the hospital's
forecourt from a first-floor window, thought she
looked charming, and after a moment excused himself from the group of doctors around him and went
down to the entrance to meet her.

He greeted her with his usual calm, enquired as to
whether she had enjoyed her day and walked her to
the imposing room where the reception was being
held. There were a great many people there, and she
recognised quite a few of them. Ethel was there too,
and came to meet them.

'You found your way,' she observed. 'Have you
had a nice look at the shops?'

'Lovely. I like Utrecht.'

'We must see what you think of Cologne,' remarked the doctor, and drew them both into a group of people Beatrice had already met. Waiters were sliding in and out of the groups with trays of drinks and dishes of canapés, and presently Ethel wandered off and Oliver escorted her around the room, making sure that she met as many people as possible. He seemed to know everyone there, and when in a quiet moment she remarked upon that he said, 'Well, I have been here several times during the last few years.'

'Have you been a consultant for a long time?'

He smiled slowly. 'Let me see, I'm thirty-seven. Six years or so.'

'You're clever, aren't you? I said that once before, but I can't help remembering that when you are like this...'

'Like what?' He sounded amused.

'Grey suit, silk tie and—and a bit remote.'

'Ah, I must remedy that, mustn't I? When we get home and I have time, we must climb the hill together again—I promise you that I won't be in the least bit remote.'

Beatrice went faintly pink. She felt a pleasant little thrill, unfortunately doused by the arrival of a powerful-looking man with a fierce moustache who wrung Oliver's hand and, on being introduced as the Burgermeester of Utrecht, clasped hers and addressed her as 'little lady'—which, while not in the least appropriate, did much for her self-esteem.

'Charming, charming. You will come again, both of you, of course!'

'Of course,' agreed the doctor blandly. 'We shall look forward to that.'

Alone again, Beatrice asked, 'Why did you say that? About us coming again?'

Two elderly gentlemen were bearing down upon them; Oliver turned to greet them. 'But we will come again,' he said over his shoulder, and then, 'This is the hospital director and a very important man...'

After that there was no more opportunity to talk together and presently they said their goodbyes, found Ethel and went out to the forecourt where the cars were parked.

They talked of their forthcoming visit to Cologne, the morning's reception and of the various people they had met while they ate their lunch. The restaurant was full, and the doctor paused to greet several people as they went to their table, his arm on hers, and invariably they all expressed the hope that they would see them again. 'We shall be over in London in the autumn,' said one serious-looking professor, lunching with his wife. 'You must both come and dine.'

Beatrice was tempted to point out to Oliver that the various acquaintances who had expressed a hope that they would meet again—and that included her— were mistaken, but she didn't want to say so in front of Ethel. She kept quiet, ate her lobster thermidor and a towering confection of ice-cream, chocolate and whipped cream, and joined in the small talk.

It was three o'clock when the doctor edged the Rolls out into the city's traffic. They drove south, over the Rhine, crossing into Germany at Emmerich and following the road through Xanten to Krefeld, a large industrial town, a blot on the scenery round about them. Presently they stopped in a village and had tea, and Beatrice studied the map.

'There are several roads,' remarked Beatrice, 'all going to Cologne.'

'Yes. We shall go back on another route so that you get a chance to see as much as possible of this part of Germany.'

'The Rhine must be lovely.'

'Oh, it is, but you need to get past Bonn. Last time we came I had a day to spare, and we drove along the Rhine, past the Lorelei Rock. Unfortunately there will be no time to go anywhere on this trip.'

'Did you—that is, was your fiancée with you?'

She was looking at the map and didn't see the look which passed between her companions. 'No, but Ethel was.'

'It was gorgeous,' enthused Ethel, and enlarged upon the beauties of the Rhine at some length, until they got up to go.

The doctor drove on, turning off the main road to go through Zons, a small medieval town about twenty miles from Cologne. It was a charming place, and he obligingly parked the car for a little while so

that Beatrice could stroll through its streets with
Ethel on one side and him on the other, pointing out
the ancient buildings.

Cologne cathedral was visible before they had a
clear view of the city, its twin towers soaring up-
wards, and once they reached its heart it seemed to
overshadow the old houses with their gabled roofs.
But there were a great many modern buildings too,
and the streets were bustling with people and traffic.
Beatrice didn't think, at first glance, that she was
going to like it as much as she had liked Utrecht,
although the sight of the great cathedral was awe-
inspiring. The hotel, close to it, was awe-inspiring
too, and very grand. She gave it a somewhat doubtful
look as they stopped before its splendid entrance, and
Oliver said, 'I agree with you—very five-star, isn't
it? Not quite what I would have chosen, but of course
everything is arranged beforehand. At least it is central, and I have no doubt very comfortable.'

Which it was. Their rooms were on the first floor
again but at the back of the hotel, overlooking a quiet
square. They were opulently furnished, and Beatrice
and Ethel poked their noses into every corner of
them. 'I only hope that my little black number will
be up to standard,' said Ethel with a giggle.

It seemed they were to follow the same routine as
they had in Utrecht, and presently they went down
to the brilliantly lit bar and found Oliver waiting for
them. 'The surroundings call for nothing less than
champagne cocktails,' he observed, 'and I can only

hope that you are both hungry, for the menu is sumptuous.'

The restaurant, when they reached it, was even more brilliantly lit than the bar. Beatrice took her seat at the window-table reserved for the doctor and studied the menu. It was indeed sumptuous. She chose cold watercress soup with cream, and then worked her way through the elaborate menu; far too much choice, she reflected, but perhaps the Hotel Excelsior Ernst had to live up to its five stars. Then she settled for grilled sole with a white wine sauce, straw potatoes and *petits pois à la flamande*. Ethel chose chicken, and the doctor, without looking at the menu, asked for fillet steak with *vigneronne*. The waiter looked quite upset as he removed the menus, their choice was obviously too modest, although the wine waiter treated the doctor's choice of a bottle of red burgundy for himself and a bottle of Chablis Grand Cru for the ladies with the respect it deserved. Beatrice, tasting hers, declared it to be a very nice wine, unaware that it had cost more than twenty pounds a bottle.

She and Ethel chose the same sweet, a light peach tart which they pronounced to be perfection, but the doctor took his choice of the cheeseboard. Beatrice would have been content to have sat over coffee, but Oliver had some work for Ethel, so she declared herself tired and wishful of an early night and, armed with the guide to Cologne with which Oliver had thoughtfully provided her, left the restaurant with every sign of eagerness to get to her room. The three of them stood in the foyer for a moment, then Ethel went away to get some papers she needed and Beatrice made to follow her up the staircase. Oliver's large hand on her arm checked her.

'I shall have very little time to myself tomorrow,' he told her, 'but if you don't mind eating a snack lunch in a hurry, we'll have it together.' He frowned in thought. 'Now, where shall we meet? Somewhere you can find easily.' He smiled. 'The cathedral, of course. Inside the main door and the centre nave. Half-past twelve?'

'Oh, that would be nice. Are you sure that you can spare the time?'

He smiled again. 'Oh, indeed I can. Goodnight, Beatrice. I don't want to say it, but I must.' He picked up her hand and kissed it gently. 'Sleep well.'

Undressing slowly, Beatrice did her best to sort out her thoughts. They were a bit muddled; Oliver was beginning to loom rather large in them and, while she told herself that it was gratitude that she felt for him, she couldn't deny that he attracted her. 'I shan't sleep,' she declared to her reflection in the ornate looking-glass as she slapped cream on to her face.

She got into bed and slept within seconds.

Breakfast was a businesslike meal and brisk. Oliver was brisk too, while Ethel perused her notebook. They got up to go long before she was finished, and

Oliver said, 'Don't forget to be in the cathedral, half-past twelve.'

He got up and was gone before she could say a word.

She spent the morning finding her way around the city. There was a street of shops close to the hotel, and she wandered down to it, looking at the windows and doing sums in her head, changing German marks into pounds and deciding that everything was rather expensive. All the same, she was tempted to buy a leather belt for Ella and a silk scarf for her mother. She still had an hour to spare by the time she reached the cathedral, so she found a small café and had coffee and tidied herself. Then she sat for a little while, looking around her at the vast place. It was magnificent, and presently she got up and walked around, clutching her guidebook and stopping every few yards to consult it. It took quite a long time. She was surprised when she looked at her watch to see that it was very nearly half-past twelve, and she hurried back to the central nave. She was at the wrong end, of course, so she hurried towards the great door, and half-way there was brought to a standstill by Oliver's hand.

'I would have waited for you, Beatrice,' he said, half laughing.

'Yes—well...' she was breathless with her haste and the pleasure of seeing him again '...I thought I was late, and you said you wouldn't have much time.'

'There's a coffee-shop in an arcade near here. I dare say we can get something there. I'll be finished by six o'clock; the three of us can meet in the bar at seven o'clock. Tomorrow evening there's a dinner at the town hall; you'll come, won't you? And the following day I shall be busy until the afternoon—there's a reception at three o'clock. I'll fetch you from the hotel. We'll leave for Copenhagen the next morning.'

While she was listening he was steering her out of the cathedral and through the crowds outside into a nearby arcade to the coffee-shop. It was almost full and very noisy, but he found a table against one wall and sat her down. 'Coffee—and what would you like to eat?'

She looked at the counter behind them, loaded with rich cakes and pastries and a variety of breads and rolls. She said, 'I'll get fat—all that cream... I'll have a *brioche* and butter. I'm not hungry.'

He gave the order. 'Nor I, although I believe that if I were to enter your mother's kitchen at this moment and smell bacon sizzling in its pan I'd be famished.'

Over their simple meal he told her about the journey to Copenhagen. 'Hanover, Hamburg, Lubeck and Copenhagen.'

'It's miles—why don't you fly?' she wanted to know.

'Driving gives me a respite between one lecture and another. You don't find it too tiring?'

'Me, heavens, no! I'm loving every moment.' She added, 'I liked Utrecht.'

'One of my favourite seminars! Did you do any shopping here?'

'A belt for Ella and a scarf for my mother. Everything's rather expensive.'

'I dare say you'll find something more to your taste in Copenhagen. Brussels isn't cheap, either.' He glanced at his watch. 'Have you something to do this afternoon?'

'I thought I'd just wander round. I suppose I couldn't come to your lecture?'

'Of course you can, though it will be in German. You can sit with Ethel, she'll be delighted.'

Beatrice got to her feet. 'Oh, thank you. You don't mind? Ethel has to take notes, doesn't she?'

'Oh, yes, but not all the time.'

They walked together through the crowded streets and down a narrow side street bordered on one side by the hospital where he was to lecture.

'There's a side door,' he told her, and ushered her through a narrow archway and into a covered passage which led to the main building. The passages seemed endless to her, and the faint hospital smells revived memories of her father's illness; she was relieved when he opened a swing door and she found herself standing with him at the side of a large assembly hall.

'Ethel's sitting near the front. There she is.' He

led the way down the aisle and tapped his secretary on the shoulder.

She turned a beaming face to them. 'Beatrice—oh, how nice, have you come to hear the lecture?' She turned a suddenly severe face on the doctor. 'You are cutting it fine, doctor—barely ten minutes. Have you your notes?'

'In my pocket. Ethel, take Beatrice to tea when I've finished. I'll see you both back at the hotel.'

He disappeared and Beatrice sat down beside Ethel. 'Do you understand German as well as being able to speak it? I mean, the kind of German Oliver uses when he lectures?'

'Bless you, yes. My father was in the army, he was stationed here for years and I went to school here. It comes in handy. Do you want me to translate?'

Beatrice shook her head. 'Even in English I don't suppose I'd understand the half of it. I'd just like to listen.'

Ethel gave her a quick look. 'Yes. Well, he's got a lovely voice.'

Oliver looked frightfully different somehow when he came on to the platform. Remote and so assured, and at the same time self-effacing. She understood nothing of what he was saying, of course, but he spoke fluently and without haste, and several times the crowded hall burst into laughter. The lecture lasted a long time, and Beatrice allowed her thoughts to wander. Would the girl he was going to marry

accompany him on these lecture tours? she wondered. And later on, when they had children, would
they stay at home and she with them, or would there
be a nanny, a nice, old-fashioned type, so that his
wife could travel with him? Or perhaps he would
give up lecturing... They wouldn't stay at the Hotel
Excelsior Ernst, though; they would go to small,
quite quiet places and spend as much time as possible
together.

Ethel's hissed whisper, 'He's finished the lecture,
now they ask questions,' brought her back to her sur-
roundings, and she sat listening and watching with
awe as Ethel scrawled shorthand on page after page
of her notebook.

'Do you have to type all that?' she whispered.

Ethel nodded. 'I get paid an enormous salary,' she
added.

'You must be worth every penny of it.'

Ethel nodded again, entirely without conceit.

Finally it was all over and they slipped out into
the street, and Ethel led the way to a coffee-shop not
far from the hotel.

'It had better be coffee. Shall we have one of those
enormous cakes?'

They had a delightful hour, the two of them, discussing clothes and make-up and the tour so far.
'Very successful,' observed Ethel. 'But then, they always are.' But she didn't talk about Oliver, and Beatrice knew that even if she asked questions about
him she would be very politely side-tracked. Ethel

might earn a splendid salary, but that had nothing to do with her loyalty to the doctor. Discretion, thought Beatrice, was probably her middle name.

They didn't hurry back to the hotel, but stopped to examine the shop windows. In the foyer, Ethel said, 'You'll be all right on your own for an hour? I've these notes to type.'

'And I've kept you from them,' said Beatrice contritely. 'I'm sorry.'

'Don't be. It was fun. There's only one lecture tomorrow, so I shall have time to get my typing done. There's a lecture on the following morning, but I'm free in the afternoon and we don't leave till the day after that.'

Dinner that evening was a light-hearted affair. Getting ready for bed later, Beatrice reflected that Oliver was a delightful companion with a quiet sense of humour which was never unkind. She went to sleep confident that the next day would be just as delightful as that day had been.

In this she was disappointed, for after breakfast Oliver went away and she saw nothing of him until the late afternoon; she filled her day with more sightseeing and window-shopping, and after a late cup of tea with him and Ethel she went away to dress for the evening. It would be the satin skirt and blouse again.

There were far more people at the dinner than there had been in Utrecht. She found herself between two youngish men who spoke impeccable English

and were flatteringly attentive. Oliver sat across the
table from her with a handsome, well-dressed woman
on either side of him, and although he caught her eye
and smiled at her once or twice he seemed to be quite
content where he was. She felt a surge of peevishness, and responded rather more warmly than she had
intended to the younger of the two men.

The dinner lasted a long time and there was a great
deal of it. They rose from the table at last after a
series of speeches—one from Oliver—and stood
around in the adjoining room, talking. Oliver had
joined her once more, and her dinner partner, still
with her, asked politely, 'You are engaged to be married to the good doctor?'

'Heavens, no!' said Beatrice, and added coldly,
'Dr Latimer is a family friend.'

'Of course. A pity that you cannot stay longer in
our beautiful city. I would have given myself the
pleasure of showing you its various splendid buildings.'

Beatrice, well aware that Oliver's eyes were on her
face, smiled with charm and allowed her eyelashes
to sweep down on to her cheeks and up again. For
some reason, she wanted to annoy him. 'That would
have been delightful. If I should return, perhaps you
will ask me again.'

He wished her goodbye and kissed her hand, and
she smiled again very sweetly. She didn't like him
very much, but since they were unlikely to see each
other again that didn't matter. She enlarged on his

charming manner as they went back to the hotel, until Oliver spoilt it all by remarking placidly, 'A nice enough fellow—married with four children and a very stout wife.'

Beatrice swept through the foyer ahead of him and stopped at the foot of the staircase. 'You could have said so hours ago,' she pointed out with a snap.

'My dear girl, who am I to put a damper on your pleasures?'

'Oh, pooh.' She tossed her head. 'Goodnight, Oliver.'

She debated whether to have a headache the next afternoon and not go with him to the reception, but in this she was forestalled by his unexpected appearance at the table where she and Ethel were having lunch.

'I'll come for you both,' he told them, 'and if you feel a headache coming on, Beatrice, take a couple of Panadol and lie down for an hour.'

He smiled at them both and wandered away again, and Ethel said, 'He never seems to get tired. Have you got a headache? You'd better go and rest, and I'll call you in good time.'

It was difficult to be annoyed with Oliver for more than a few minutes, for the simple reason that he ignored the fact that one was cross in the first place. She and Ethel were ready when he came for them and, truth to tell, she enjoyed the reception. Everyone there was very hearty and friendly, and the little cakes were delicious. Although Oliver left her from

time to time, he was always at her elbow just when
he was needed. The evening passed with the three of
them enjoying another elaborate dinner while they
discussed their stay in Cologne and their journey
north on the following day.

'I've allowed two days to get to Copenhagen,' explained Oliver casually. 'We shall go as far as
Salzhausen, just south of Hamburg, tomorrow and do
the rest of the journey on the following day.'

He glanced at Ethel. 'Ethel fixed things up at the
hotel there. It's in the country, the Luneburg Heath—
and it's old and quiet. A nice change for us all. I
thought we might leave soon after breakfast in the
morning and get there for a late lunch.'

'I've got the notes for Copenhagen,' Ethel reminded him. 'Would you like them now?'

'Why not, if you are not too tired.'

It seemed the right moment for Beatrice to declare
herself tired and ready for bed. She got up when
Ethel did, and the doctor got up too, strolling with
her across the foyer, with Ethel hurrying ahead to get
the papers he wanted. At the staircase he came to a
halt.

'You stole quite a few hearts today,' he told her,
smiling. He touched her cheek gently with one finger.
'You're a little pale; a few hours in the country will
do you good. You're not unhappy?'

'No—no, I'm not. How could I be? I'm having
such a lovely time. I'll never be able to thank you
enough.'

He only smiled again. 'Goodnight, Beatrice.' He took her hand and held it for a few moments. 'Sleep well.'

He really was a nice person, she thought sleepily as she jumped into bed. Although she was never quite sure what he was really thinking.

It was raining as they left Cologne, but by the time they reached Hanover the sun was shining again and they stopped at a wayside café for coffee. They didn't linger over it, and by one o'clock they were crossing the heath to stop before the hotel. It was of red brick and thatched, and once inside they were transported into the sixteenth century. Not that it lacked a single modern luxury, skilfully tucked away behind the old and beautiful furniture and the ancient walls. Beatrice rotated slowly round the room she was to have; she was enthralled. This, she decided, was the real Germany, away from the bright lights and the chandeliers. They went presently for lunch: local fish, a splendid salad and a rich tart for afters, helped along by the wine the doctor chose. They had coffee in the lounge, and since Ethel declared that she wanted to work on her notes Oliver and Beatrice took themselves off for a walk.

It was a quiet countryside, and unspoilt. They walked for hours, talking when they felt like it, at ease with each other, and they went back for coffee and cakes and a leisurely hour sitting outside in the evening light.

It was nice to give the blouse and skirt and the

printed dress a rest. Beatrice got into one of her
pretty summer dresses, wound her hair into a chignon
and wandered downstairs, where she found Oliver
waiting for her.

'Ethel isn't quite ready,' she told him. 'She said
ten minutes, if you don't mind.'

'We'll have a drink while we are waiting and have
a look at the menu.'

Beatrice worried her way through the German.
'Why is this a *Romantik* hotel?' she asked.

'A chain of hotels throughout Europe, all living up
to a certain standard. Candles on the tables, good
food, comfortable rooms and so on, so that those
with romantic intentions can indulge them.'

'Oh, but other people stay at them? I mean, people
who aren't being romantic?'

'Naturally. You need only consider the three of us
to prove it.' A remark uttered in such bland tones
that she could think of nothing in reply.

The food was excellent. They dined at leisure, and
Beatrice and Ethel went to their beds soon after.
Tomorrow would be another long day.

They left after an excellent breakfast, circumventing Hamburg and crossing into Denmark, driving up
the road to Kolding and then on to the island of Fu-
nen, crossing on the ferry to Korsor, across the island
of Zeeland and finally reaching Copenhagen. They
hadn't hurried, and it was late afternoon by the time
the doctor stopped at a hotel overlooking the harbour.
'Myhavn 71,' he told her, 'another *Romantik* hotel,

and a good deal quieter than the Royal or the D'Angleterre.'

It was charming none the less, and had a quiet air of luxury borne out by the rooms into which they were shown. Beatrice unpacked, showered and changed into another summer dress and went down to the foyer. Ethel and Oliver were already there, sitting at a table, and Ethel's notebook was open. She closed it now and the three of them talked in the pleasant, lazy way people do when they have been travelling all day, and presently they went in to dinner.

The menu was French, but by way of a speciality there was a vast centre table laid out with smorgasbord, and with their appetites nicely whetted they went on to lobster and then strawberries and finally coffee, strong and dark and unlimited.

Beatrice, watching the harbour beyond her bedroom window before she got into bed, felt contentment flooding her. Tomorrow she would be on her own until the early afternoon, but she had a map the ever-thoughtful doctor had got for her, and he had promised that he would take her to see the Little Mermaid before they both went to the evening reception at the University. 'Only an hour or so; we shall be back at the hotel by seven o'clock. We'll have dinner and we'll all go to the Tivoli Gardens,' he had told her. 'The dinner will be on the second day, but I shan't need Ethel in the morning, so the pair of you can go shopping or sightseeing.'

The next two days were every bit as delightful as
she had known they would be. The shops were splendid and everyone spoke English. She had spent her
first morning prowling around the department stores,
and in the afternoon she had driven with Oliver along
the road by the water to see the Little Mermaid—a
wistful little figure, but disappointingly smaller than
she had imagined she would be.

The reception had been a good deal livelier than
the one at Cologne, and there hadn't been the
language difficulty; she had loved every minute of it.
And on the second day she and Ethel had poked
around the shops, buying trinkets and small figurines
of porcelain before going back to the hotel and having lunch, while they discussed their visit to the Tivoli Gardens the previous evening. It had been marvellous, they agreed, and the doctor had been more
than generous, paying for them to take part in its
attractions and waiting patiently while they tried their
luck in the shooting galleries and gazed open-
mouthed at the firework display.

The dinner had been rather solemn to begin with,
but soon livened up. Beatrice, in the blouse and skirt
once more, had been glad to find Oliver sitting beside
her, while on her other side was a young Danish
doctor who knew England well and moreover admired her quite openly.

She had been annoyed when the doctor had remarked upon that as they drove back to the hotel.
'Turn all heads, don't you?' he'd remarked cheer-

fully. 'I wonder who it will be in Brussels.' She had told him tartly that she neither knew nor cared, and he had chuckled to himself which had annoyed her still more. But on the whole they had got on very well indeed; she had come to miss him when he wasn't there.

The Rolls made light of the long drive to Brussels and they stopped on the German-Belgian border and had a leisurely lunch at a country restaurant, then took a stroll for half an hour before getting back into the car. Their hotel was in the centre of the city, an elegant building with the best shops close by, but, as the doctor pointed out, there were only two lectures to give in Brussels and both on the same day. 'So make the most of it,' he told Beatrice. 'There will be a luncheon at the hospital tomorrow and I would like you to come to that with me. I have another lecture in the afternoon, but we could go out in the evening if you would like that, while Ethel gets the last of the typing done.'

So she had spent the morning looking at the shops but buying very little; some chocolates for her sisters, a tie for her father and a pretty brooch for her mother, as well as biscuits for Mrs Perry and the Sharpe family. And by then it was time to pretty herself for the luncheon and go down to wait for Oliver.

She enjoyed herself, although she had felt a little doubtful of it. But it gave her an opportunity to air her French, which was really rather good, and the food was delicious. She spent the afternoon packing

her things and went down to the foyer, refreshed by
a tray of tea in her room and a leisurely bath. Ethel
was already there with the doctor, and after dinner
the three of them went out. Oliver seemed to know
just where to go, but then she would have been surprised if he didn't; they had drinks at a fashionable
café, walked a little, had coffee at another hotel and
then strolled back.

'Well, there goes our last evening,' observed Oliver placidly. 'Back to the grindstone tomorrow. We
shall leave soon after breakfast—we'll go over from
Ostend.'

He bade them goodnight in the foyer, not giving
Beatrice a chance to tell him how much she had enjoyed herself. Indeed, his manner was so remotely
kind that she hesitated to do more than wish him
goodnight. She went to bed feeling dissatisfied and
vaguely unhappy. Somehow or other she would con-
trive to thank him properly before she reached home.
She had much to thank him for, she reflected; she
had only been away for two weeks, but already Colin
seemed like a character in a book she had forgotten
she had read.

CHAPTER EIGHT

IT WAS raining when they left Brussels, and it was still raining when they reached England and drove westwards. They stopped in Ightham at the Town House, a restaurant with a high reputation and an imaginative menu, and had lunch before Oliver joined the motorway and presently the A303, explaining that it would be easier and quicker if he were to take Beatrice home first and then drive back to London, first to Ethel's flat and then to his home.

'Will you stay in London?' Beatrice made her voice casual.

'For a week at least. There will be a backlog of patients, as well as urgent new cases. Ethel is to have a well-earned holiday—I only hope the temp they send will work half as hard. I'm lost without her.'

Ethel had heard him from the back seat. 'Well, if it's that Miss Duffield who came last year, she was most efficient...'

'She terrified me.' He glanced at Beatrice. 'Do you suppose your mother would give us tea? Then we shan't need to stop on our way home.'

'Of course she will. I sent her a card days ago, and told her to expect us any time after four o'clock.'

'Splendid.' After that, they didn't talk much, and

Ethel dozed off. The doctor glanced in his mirror and said quietly, 'She must be worn out; she never misses a trick. She certainly deserves a week off.' He gave Beatrice a sideways glance. 'And you, Beatrice? What will you do now you're home again?'

'Help Father, and there's always heaps to do in the village—coffee mornings and the church bazaar and the children's summer outing, and if anyone's away or ill I help out with meals on wheels.'

'The mind boggles.'

Come to think of it, thought Beatrice, my mind boggles too. It never used to, I'm getting discontented... She said defiantly, 'Oh, I like doing those things.'

He murmured politely, 'Of course, you will get married. Is Kathy back from her honeymoon?'

And after that they talked about Kathy and Ella and Carol in general, and although Beatrice tried to lead the talk back to his own plans he gave nothing away, so that she was forced to fall back on dull topics like the weather and the likelihood of there being a good harvest.

He stopped before her home door soon after five o'clock, and it was flung open instantly to allow Mrs Browning, Ella and Carol with Knotty to surge out to greet them.

'Come in,' cried Mrs Browning, embracing Beatrice, shaking hands with Oliver and Ethel, and urging them indoors. 'Isn't this delightful? And I'm longing to hear all about the trip, but I suppose you won't have time to tell me. Tea's ready. Ethel—you don't mind if I call you Ethel?—Beatrice will take you upstairs. Oliver, go straight into the sitting-room. I'll fetch the tea-tray.'

He went with her to the kitchen and took the tray from her. 'Young Wood has gone?' he asked.

'Yes, a week ago. But there are several letters…' Mrs Browning looked at him with troubled eyes.

'Don't worry too much. I am almost sure that Beatrice has got over him—he hadn't gone very deep, you know. Let her have the letters.'

'If you say so, Oliver.' Mrs Browning picked up a plate of scones and started back to the sitting-room.

'You don't mind if Ethel and I leave within the hour? She is tired and I am faced with an out-patients at nine o'clock in the morning.' He put the tray on a table. 'I'd like to take a quick look at Mr Browning before I go. He's well?'

'Yes. Mr Sharpe is just right as a partner, and they get on famously. He'll be glad to have Beatrice back, though Ella's been very good.'

'If Beatrice should marry, someone will have to take her place.'

'Yes, but there isn't anyone at the moment.'

Mrs Browning was arranging plates, and didn't see Oliver's face, only heard his quiet, 'Not at the moment, no.'

Ethel and Beatrice came in, and a minute later Ella and Mr Browning, and they sat round the open windows talking about their journey and eating Mrs

Browning's scones and cakes. 'What a lovely tea,' said Ethel, and passed her cup for the third time.

The men went away presently, and Beatrice took Ethel for a quick look at the clinic. When they got back to the house, Oliver was waiting for them and goodbyes were said without delay.

'I still haven't had the chance...' began Beatrice, her well-rehearsed speech of thanks ready on her tongue, but never to be uttered, it seemed, for Oliver shook hands briefly, wished her a brisk goodbye and ushered Ethel into the front seat of the car. She watched him drive away. Now she would have to write a thank-you letter, for she had no idea when she would see him again. She stopped suddenly as they turned to go back indoors. She would have to see him again, she couldn't bear the thought of not doing so—just once more and then never again. He was going to be married to a nice girl who trusted him, and it was just a hideous quirk of fate that she had fallen in love with him.

Her mother, waiting for her to go indoors, said briskly, 'Are you coming in, darling?'

Beatrice found a nice normal voice to say, 'It's such a lovely evening now, I'm going to walk round the garden with Knotty.'

She walked aimlessly for some time, thinking about Oliver and trying to decide when she had fallen in love. She had always liked him from the moment they had met, and she had never thought of him as a stranger, but to pinpoint the moment when she knew that she loved him was impossible. It was because he had gone away so quickly and casually that the fact had been brought home to her now.

'And there is absolutely nothing to be done about it,' she added unhappily to Knotty. 'What a mess I have made of things, haven't I?'

She went back indoors presently and spent the rest of the evening giving her mother and father and Ella a detailed report on her travels.

'How very exciting,' remarked Mrs Browning, 'and to think that Oliver goes on these trips at least once a year. I'm not surprised he hasn't married; he can't have had much time to do so.'

'Well, he's going to soon.'

'Is he, dear? That will be nice.'

Her mother, thought Beatrice peevishly, could at times be quite infuriating.

It wasn't difficult to slip back into her usual working days again, and she welcomed the fact that they were busier than usual. It was only at the end of the day, in her own room, that she allowed herself to think about Oliver, wondering what he was doing and where he was. Somehow nothing else mattered; she had torn up Colin's letters without opening them, to her mother's secret satisfaction, and there was certainly no room in her mind for any thoughts of him. The week went past, and very nearly a second one, before something happened to disrupt her busy, unexciting days.

A letter came from Great-Aunt Sybil. Miss Moore

was taking a week's holiday—for urgent family reasons—and, since Aunt Sybil could on no account be expected to manage without a companion, Beatrice was invited to spend a week in her place. 'Invited' wasn't perhaps the right word, the invitation was worded more in the form of a command but, as Mrs Browning said, the poor old thing was to be pitied.

'Why?' asked Beatrice, not best pleased at the summons.

'Well, dear, no one loves her, do they? We do our duty by her; your father manages her shares and things for her, and I go and see her once a month and you fill in gaps, but none of us likes doing it.'

'How right, Mother. But I'll go, if only to keep the peace. Nothing much can happen in a week.'

She went away to pack her bag, happily unaware that she was quite mistaken.

Great-Aunt Sybil gave her a grudging welcome. Miss Moore had already gone, leaving a neat list of things which had to be done for Beatrice. They were innumerable, and Beatrice, reading it, saw that the week ahead would be a difficult one, given that she wasn't Miss Moore in the first place, and furthermore would have to contend with her great-aunt's ill humour because Miss Moore wasn't there.

The first day went well enough; Beatrice, anxious to please, wound wool, fetched spectacles, read aloud and listened with an intelligent face and half an ear to Miss Browning's forceful opinions of the government. She had heard most of them before, and beyond a suitable, 'oh', or 'I see', she was free to think her own thoughts of Oliver.

But on the second day she blotted her copy-book badly by forgetting the pills that her great-aunt took for her indigestion; worse, forgetting where they were. 'Miss Moore,' pronounced Miss Browning in disagreeably loud tones, 'forgets nothing. If it were not for her, I should very likely be lying in my grave.'

'Oh, well,' said Beatrice cheerfully, 'it's only for a week, Aunt Sybil, and think how much you'll enjoy seeing her again.'

'You are still an impertinent young woman,' said Great-Aunt Sybil.

It was difficult not to be bored; the weather had changed as it so often did in an English summer, to drizzling rain and brief snatches of sun which lasted long enough for one to go out of doors and get caught in the next shower. Beatrice played card games with her aunt, read the papers from cover to cover, and thought about Oliver.

There was a thunderstorm on the fourth day of her visit; it rumbled all day and then, as night fell, reached a crescendo of noise, interlarded by flashes of blue lightning which Beatrice didn't like at all. None the less, Miss Browning elected to go to her bed at the usual hour, and Beatrice, left on her own since Mrs Shadwell had retired to her room too, decided that bed might be the best place. She pulled the curtains close, turned on all the lights and presently got into bed, where she dozed off over a book. When she woke an hour later the storm had died away; indeed, it was too quiet, with not a breath of wind and no sound of traffic.

She got up, switched off the lights, got back into bed and closed her eyes. She was asleep at once and didn't wake again until the rising sun woke her. It was six o'clock or thereabouts, and a lovely morning. To go to sleep again would be a waste of time. She got up, put on her dressing-gown, slipped into her slippers and went quietly downstairs, intent on making a cup of tea before Mrs Shadwell got down.

She was half-way down the stairs when she heard a faint sound. A drawer opening or being shut? A door closing? She paused, frowning. Mrs Shadwell never came down until just after seven o'clock, and her great-aunt remained in her room until she had breakfasted. It might be the milkman, but the sounds had come from the front of the house. Beatrice, not a nervous type, tied her dressing-gown girdle more tightly, tossed her mane of hair over her shoulders and trod softly down to the hall.

The front door was still locked and chained, but the drawing-room door was ajar. She pushed it open and peered round it. A man was standing in front of the handsome bow-fronted cabinet where Miss Browning's splendid collection of antique silver was housed. He had a case open beside him and was picking and choosing the best pieces.

Fright held Beatrice silent for a moment and then

indignation took over. 'Put everything back at once,' she said in a voice which shook only very slightly. 'I'm going to call the police.'

Even as she uttered these brave words, she saw that the french window at the other side of the house behind him was open, and since the telephone was at the other end of the room he had a distinct advantage—which he took. Snatching up the case, shedding christening spoons, silver dishes, goblets and some really fine snuff boxes as he did so, he ran out. Beatrice went after him. Never mind the phone; she was a splendid runner and he was a heavily built man, lumbering across the garden which gave on to an alley-way at the back of the house. But half-way there, with her in hot pursuit, he turned, to run down the side of the house and jump the little iron railing and dash along the pavement. Beatrice, hard on his heels, wished in vain for the milkman, someone going to work—anyone. Characters in books always cried, 'Stop, thief!' but she had no breath for that; she was gaining, but once out of the square there were several narrow roads where he could get out of sight.

Oliver, on his way to spend a couple of quiet days at his home, saw the man first and then Beatrice, her hair flying, dressing-gown all anyhow, tearing along like a girl possessed. If he had been uncertain as to what was happening, the sight of a small Georgian coffee-pot at the side of the road would have helped him to understand the situation. But he didn't need

silver coffee-pots; with a snort of laughter he over-
took the man, got out of his car, knocked him down
and then put a well-shod foot on him.

'Hello,' said Beatrice, and flung her hair out of the
way and tugged her dressing-gown into decency. 'He
was stealing the silver.'

The doctor smiled in his nice calm way. 'I thought
that might be it. Get in the car, my dear, and phone
the police, and stay there until they come.'

She turned to go. 'You always come,' she said,
and his smile widened.

All he said was, 'Run along now.'

She sat obediently while the police came and put
the man in their car and asked her a lot of questions.
She answered them in her sensible way, and looked
astonished when the police sergeant warned her in a
fatherly fashion not to go running after thieves again.

'He could have turned nasty, miss,' he told her.
She forebore from telling him that Great-Aunt Sybil
could turn nasty too, especially if she had come
downstairs and found her cabinets rifled. On the
whole, she thought, she preferred the burglar.

She would be required to make a statement, said
the pleasant police sergeant, but later in the day. He
cast an eye over her appearance. 'You'll need to go
home and have a nice cup of tea, miss,' he told her
kindly. 'A bit of a shock it must have been.'

Oliver was leaning against the car's bonnet. 'I'll
see her safely back, Sergeant. I'm a friend of the
family and I know her aunt.'

So presently he got into the car and drove the short distance to Miss Browning's house, its quiet dignity disturbed by a police car parked on the street outside and a police officer standing at the door, while another one pottered up and down the square, retrieving teaspoons, snuff boxes and a badly dented teapot...

Inside there was a good deal of noise and confusion. Loud voices in the drawing-room seemed the signal for them to peer round the door, to see Aunt Sybil, clad in a magnificent dressing-gown, sitting very upright in a chair before the almost empty cabinet. Mrs Shadwell was standing behind her, wringing her hands, and the daily girl who came in to help stood just inside the door. She looked round at Beatrice and Oliver as they went in and exclaimed, 'Well, I never...' in a loud, excited voice, so that Great-Aunt Sybil and her housekeeper gave up contemplating the cabinet and turned round.

'Beatrice,' Miss Browning's voice trembled a little with shock, 'you are undressed, I am told that you have been in the square, I am deeply mortified.'

Beatrice, without realising it, clutched Oliver's hand. 'So sorry, Aunt Sybil, but I saw this man making off with the silver. I'm sure you'd have been a good deal more mortified if I'd let him go without trying to stop him.'

'You could have called the police instead of tearing round Wilton like a demented...'

The doctor stopped her, a cutting edge to his calm

voice which would have silenced a howling mob.
'Miss Browning, you do not appear to understand the
situation. Beatrice very bravely challenged the thief,
and since the telephone was out of reach, did what
any person with a spark of courage would have done:
tried to stop him. I find your attitude utterly incom-
prehensible. You should be unendingly grateful to
her.'

He flung a large arm round Beatrice's shoulders.
'I shall take her home as soon as she is dressed and
has packed her bag.'

Great-Aunt Sybil went a delicate puce, made several attempts to speak and at last said, 'Young man,
you are extremely rude…'

'I am not a young man, Miss Browning, though it
is kind of you to say so, nor am I rude.' He took his
arm from Beatrice and tapped her smartly on the
shoulder. 'Upstairs with you. Is ten minutes long
enough?'

As she went upstairs, she could hear her aunt's
voice, its rich tones vibrant with feeling. 'I shall be
alone…'

'You have these ladies—your housekeeper and her
help in the house? You do not know what it is to be
alone, Miss Browning. To sit in a small bedsitter
with not enough to eat and nothing to keep you
warm, and dependent on a neighbour's kindness if
she remembers—that is being alone!'

Beatrice paused on the stairs to listen. Her aunt
would shred him into little pieces. She was amazed

to hear her voice pitched in a lower key and almost subdued. 'Young man, I do not like you particularly, but I think that you are a good man with the courage of your convictions. Should I be taken ill—as I probably shall after this terrible shock—I shall expect you to attend me.'

Beatrice didn't wait for more, she had already wasted two minutes of the ten she had been allowed.

She dashed water on to her face, raced into her clothes, brushed her hair in a perfunctory manner and rammed everything into her bag. There were several odds and ends lying around, and her forgotten dressing-gown lying in a heap by the bed. She snatched them up and stowed them into a plastic bag she had thrown into the wastepaper basket the night before, and went downstairs.

Her aunt was still sitting in her chair; she didn't appear to have moved, and Oliver was standing by the window, looking out, his hands in his pockets. He looked, she thought, completely at ease, and she loved him all the more for it.

'A plastic bag!' exclaimed Great-Aunt Sybil. 'Must you, Beatrice? In my day, no young lady carried such a thing—why have you no luggage?'

'Well, I have Aunt, but I didn't have much time and I haven't packed very well—these are just some bits and pieces left out.'

To her utter surprise, Miss Browning observed, 'I shall give you suitable luggage for your birthday, Beatrice. Your twenty-seventh birthday.'

No girl of twenty-six likes to be reminded that she is going to be twenty-seven. Beatrice swallowed bad temper and said perkily, 'I can't wait for it; I love birthdays.'

The doctor looked over his shoulder at her and allowed a small sound to escape his lips. 'A very proper attitude,' he said approvingly. 'Shall we go? Miss Browning, the police will require a statement from Beatrice, and she will have to return here to make it. I hope and expect that you will recover anything which was taken—thanks to Beatrice.'

'Well, and you too,' said Beatrice. 'I should never have caught him if you hadn't come along.'

'An open question.' He bade Miss Browning a polite good morning, nodded to Mrs Shadwell, who was still wringing her hands, smiled at the daily help and took Beatrice's bag while she said her goodbyes in turn.

'You'll have your nice Miss Moore back in another two days,' said Beatrice cheerfully.

In the car she asked, 'Isn't it rather early for you to be driving home?' She turned to look at him, and her loving heart was touched by the tiredness of his face. 'You've been up all night,' she said.

'Well, yes, for the greater part of it. But I have the weekend to myself, and Mrs Jennings will be waiting for me with a mammoth breakfast.'

He was driving steadily, looking ahead.

'Aunt Sybil will be all right? She did say that she

simply had to have a companion. Supposing she falls ill?'

'Your Great-Aunt Sybil has a constitution of iron.' He added casually, 'You look untidy.'

Indignation swelled in her bosom. 'Of course I'm untidy. You gave me ten minutes to dress and pack, remember? And I cannot think why I did as you asked. I needed at least half an hour. I know of no other woman who would be such a fool...'

'Actually,' said the doctor at his most soothing, 'you look rather nice.'

The wind was taken out of her sails. She said contritely, 'I'm sorry, I didn't mean to snap and you're tired...'

'A couple of hours' sleep will soon put that right. I'll call for you after lunch; we can go for a drive, if you like, or go back and have tea in the garden, and lie about working up an appetite for one of Mrs Jennings' dinners.'

'I'd like that—just to sit in the garden. Aunt Sybil doesn't much care for sun and fresh air, and I've had to spend rather a lot of time indoors.'

'Two o'clock, then?'

There was a delicious smell of bacon frying as they went in to her home, and Mrs Browning was warming the teapot at the sink. She put it down rather sharply as they went in. 'Beatrice, darling, what's happened? How very untidy you are. You're not hurt? And you, Oliver, are you all right?'

'Perfectly. Beatrice surprised a burglar at her

aunt's house and gave chase—I happened to be passing by—and as I was on my way home I gave her a lift.'

'Oh, I see,' said Mrs Browning, not seeing at all. 'You both need a cup of tea and then a good breakfast, then you can tell me all about it.'

'Tea would be splendid, but I can't stay for breakfast, Mrs Jennings would never forgive me—I told her I would be home between eight and nine o'clock.'

Beatrice hadn't spoken; now she said, 'Oliver came just when I didn't know what to do next. He always comes.'

The doctor smiled gently, and her mother gave her a thoughtful look. 'Yes, dear. Sit down and drink your tea, and then have a nice hot bath and I'll make the breakfast. Oliver, you're sure you can't stay?'

He shook his head. 'I wouldn't dare. The Jenningses are hand in glove with Rosie, my housekeeper in London; between them they order my life.'

'Won't your wife mind?' asked Beatrice suddenly, and went slowly pink because he would think that she was prying.

'Oh, they'll thoroughly enjoy having someone to look after. They are worth their weight in gold.' He put down his cup. 'Thank you for the tea, Mrs Browning. If I may, I'll just take a look at Mr Browning while I'm down here. He's due for a check-up in two weeks, isn't he?'

He crossed the room to where Beatrice was sitting,

and bent and kissed her cheek. 'I'll see you at two o'clock.' He turned to her mother. 'I've asked Beatrice over to keep me company for tea and dinner.'

Mrs Browning gave him a limpid look. 'Just what she needs after several days of her Great-Aunt.' She looked at Beatrice. 'Isn't it, dear?'

Beatrice nodded, thinking about the kiss. Of course, to him it had just been a casual salute which had meant nothing to him; unfortunately it had played havoc with her heart, which seemed to be choking her and making it impossible to speak. She watched him go, and when her mother came back from seeing him to his car she got up. 'I'll go and have a bath, Mother.'

'Yes, dear. Breakfast will be about twenty minutes, and your father will be back by then, so you can tell us all about it.'

So half an hour later, bathed and dressed in the pink outfit, her hair brushed and plaited, her face nicely made-up, Beatrice sat down to her breakfast. She was allowed to make inroads into bacon and eggs before her father said, 'Well, love, tell us what happened.'

So she told. 'In your dressing-gown,' commented her mother when she had finished. 'But at that hour of the morning there wouldn't be many people about.'

'No one, Mother. And I'd forgotten what I was wearing, I just wanted to catch the man.'

'Very brave of you, darling. I think I would have crept back to bed.'

'And then Oliver came along,' said Ella, who had sat quiet, for once.

'Yes, wasn't it lucky?'

'Not luck, fate—it was meant. You keep bumping into each other, don't you? Oh, not bumping, you know what I mean. Fate throws you together.'

'You've been reading the horoscopes again,' said Beatrice in what she hoped was a light voice.

'Mother says you are having tea and dinner with him. Does he fancy you?'

Mrs Browning drew in her breath sharply and cast a warning frown at her husband, who had his mouth open to speak. It was left for Beatrice to say something. 'He is getting married very shortly. She sounds a very nice girl, and when he talks about her you can hear that he's—he's very fond of her.'

Ella was irrepressible. 'Oh, well, someone else will turn up for you. There's a letter from Colin for you; it's on the hall table.'

Beatrice who felt like crying, laughed instead. 'Ella, you're incorrigible! Shall I put on an overall and come and give you a hand with the animals? What's in, anyway?'

Half an hour later, cleaning out the small room where the smaller animals went to recover after surgery, Ella said, 'You and Oliver ought to marry— you suit each other down to the ground. And what I want to know is why, if he's so smitten with her, doesn't this girl he's going to marry ever come down to his house here? He spends almost as much time in it as he does in his London house, doesn't he? Always racing up and down the A303 at all hours of the day and night. Do you suppose she's there and no one knows?'

'If she were, I would have met her by now.' Beatrice strove to keep her voice calm. 'Besides, they're not married yet.'

Ella gave her a pitying look, 'Really, love, you're dreadfully out of date—or do I mean old-fashioned? Two of the teachers at school live with boyfriends. They're even buying a house together…'

Beatrice gently moved a sick terrier belonging to the vicar to a clean cage. 'Well, they wouldn't need to buy a house, would they? He's got two already. And I should imagine that well-known specialists in the medical profession take great care of their reputations.'

Ella hadn't finished. 'But he took you all over Europe and pretended that you were engaged. Oh, I know all about that, I asked Mother…'

Beatrice began to fill the water bowls. 'Oh, I see. Oliver did that to help me, and his fiancée knew about it. He told me that she didn't mind—that she understood. You see, Ella, it was to stop Colin thinking that I might still marry him.'

'You don't want to any more?'

'No. It was infatuation, nothing more. I dare say you know more about that than I do,' she added drily.

'I expect I do. All the same, I wish that you and Oliver...' She caught Beatrice's eye. 'You like him, don't you?'

Beatrice didn't quite meet the eye. 'Yes, he has been kind to me, and I'm grateful.'

In the car later, driving to Oliver's home, Beatrice said, 'I don't think I'll come out with you again, if you don't mind.'

'I shall mind, unless you can give me a good reason.'

She fidgeted around in her seat. 'Well, it's a bit difficult to explain. I don't think it's fair to your fiancée. I can't believe that she doesn't mind—not about me going to Utrecht and all those other places with you and Ethel, because that was just to get away from Colin, but now—today—there's no reason...'

'Today is rather an exception, isn't it?' His voice was cool. 'You had an unpleasant experience this morning. You may not realise it, but it gave you a shock; the best cure for that is to do something to take your mind off it, hence my invitation to spend an afternoon snoozing in the sun and eating one of Mrs Jennings' splendid dinners. Look upon it as medical advice, Beatrice.'

She deplored his impersonal manner, while at the same time feeling relieved at his assumption that he had offered her a kind of therapy for shock. She said, 'Very well,' in a meek voice, and made a pointless remark about the weather.

It was a pleasantly warm afternoon; they lay on

the well-cushioned loungers on the lawn behind the house, and presently Beatrice went to sleep, to wake to the gentle rattle of teacups. 'Too nice to go indoors just yet,' said Oliver. 'Be mother, will you? And tell me what plans you have for the future.'

She poured from a silver pot into wafer-thin and exquisite china cups. 'I haven't any,' she said baldly. 'Do you have sugar?'

'What—have you forgotten that already? Two lumps. Has Colin ceased to worry you?'

'Yes. I haven't thought about him for quite a while. I can't think how I ever imagined that I was in love with him.'

'One never can. But experience is valuable—it enables you to know the real thing when it comes along.'

She passed the sandwiches and didn't look at him. It was only too true in her case, and she would rather die than tell anyone, ever. She said in a wooden voice, 'I'm quite sure you're right.'

The long silence was broken by Mabel, wanting cake, and Oliver began a gentle chat about nothing much so that Beatrice was soothed into content. It wouldn't last, she knew that; sooner or later she would remember that he was going to get married to someone else, and even if he remained her friend, indeed a friend of the family, it wouldn't be the same. She bit into Mrs Jennings' walnut cake and hoped with all her heart that he would be happy.

They wandered round the garden presently, and

then strolled along to see the horses and Kate the donkey. Since it was a fine evening, they took Mabel for a walk through the open country behind the house.

Beatrice was happy; she knew it wouldn't last, but just for the moment life was everything she could ask of it. She didn't have much to say, but there didn't seem to be the need to talk. They turned for home presently, and Mrs Jennings led her away to tidy herself before dinner.

Oliver was in his drawing-room when she joined him, and they sat by the open window, watching Mabel gallop around the lawn while they had their drinks. Presently they dined. Mrs Jennings had excelled herself: a terrine of leeks and prawns in a delicate sauce, red mullet with thyme, and raspberries and cream. Beatrice did justice to the lot.

They sat over their coffee, but at length she said, 'I think I should go home now.'

Yet she felt an instant sadness at his prompt, 'Of course, you must be tired.'

'Are you going back to London on Monday?' she asked as they drove back.

'Yes, I shan't be down again for some time. There's a good deal of work for me and I have some business of my own to settle. There are certain arrangements to make before one marries.'

She was glad that she didn't need to answer that, for they had arrived at her home, and although he went in with her it was to spend a short time with her father before bidding them all goodnight in his usual pleasant manner and driving away. She didn't think that she would see him again, not as a friend, anyway. Next time he would be pleasantly impersonal, intent on checking up on her father, probably relieved that she and her tiresome problems were no longer in need of any help.

CHAPTER NINE

IT WAS only after he had been gone for an hour or more that Beatrice remembered that nothing had been said about their pseudo engagement. Since it had been announced in the paper, it would have to be revoked in the same manner. On the other hand, if Colin saw it, he might try and see her again. Perhaps Oliver intended to do nothing about it; it would be best to leave it to him.

She was grateful for the suggestion her mother made that she should go to bed rather early. 'A lot has happened today,' observed her parent, 'and you must be very tired. Your father has to go over to Telfont Evias in the morning. Perhaps you would drive him, dear? That Jersey herd there, they all have to have something done to them.'

Mrs Browning was delightfully vague about it, although her daughters suspected that she knew a great deal more about a vet's work than she appeared to.

'Yes, of course I'll go. If Father's going to be there a long time, shall I do any shopping for you in Tisbury?'

'Yes, dear. Mrs Perry wants several things, you could get them at the ironmonger's.' She glanced at her daughter's pale, sad face. 'Off to bed with you, love. Father will have to leave about eight o'clock if he's to be done by lunchtime. What a blessing Mr Sharpe is so very reliable.' She waited until Beatrice was going upstairs. 'You don't miss Colin, dear?'

'No, Mother, he doesn't mean anything any more.'

So it wasn't he who had put that unhappy look on Beatrice's face, reflected her mother, but Oliver. She frowned, for she had felt sure that he was more than interested in her. Of course, there was this girl he was going to marry. 'I'd like to see that girl with my own eyes,' muttered Mrs Browning. 'She's too good to be true, for one thing.'

The week went by, and a second followed it; Beatrice, once more back in her familiar routine, did her best not to think of Oliver and failed lamentably. She scanned the paper each morning, searching for his name among the marriage announcements, and she wrote a careful letter to Ethel, in which she took great pains not to mention the doctor, merely reiterating her enjoyment of their trip and hoping that Ethel had had a good holiday. She had a letter back in which, among other bits of news, Ethel mentioned that Oliver was working much too hard. She hadn't asked him why, it wasn't her place to do so, but she suspected the reason. This was followed by several exclamation marks which, to Beatrice's unsettled mind, implied that Ethel knew a good deal more than she intended to write.

She was in her room, making her bed, when she

looked out of the window and saw the Rolls halting smoothly in front of the house. There was a back staircase, and without stopping to think very clearly Beatrice darted from her room, sneaked down to the back door and slid away into the line of trees and shrubs beyond the field, where the convalescent horses and cows were kept. Only when she paused for breath did she wonder why she had done it. The thought uppermost in her mind was that she couldn't bear to see him again, even though she longed to do so. She fetched up against an uprooted tree and sat down on its trunk. She wasn't far away from the house; she would hear when he drove away. Presently she heard her mother's voice calling her, and then Ella, free from school for the day, shouting for her. She took no notice, they would think that she had gone for a walk or biked down to the village, and in a little while Oliver would go away.

It was almost half an hour before she heard the gentle purr of the Rolls as he left. She sat for another five minutes, just to be on the safe side, and then started back. She went a little cautiously, intent on circumventing the house and appearing from the tumbledown shed at the back of the yard where her bike was kept. She reached the corner of the clinic and poked her head cautiously round the corner.

Her view was blotted out by the vast expanse of the doctor's waistcoat within inches of her nose.

'Now, I wonder why you ran away?' he asked, pleasantly casual. 'It struck me that you were probably hiding in that convenient little patch of trees. Why?'

She stared up at him. 'Oh, dear,' she said, 'I don't know why, really I don't.' And then, being a truthful girl by nature, 'Well, I do know, but I can't tell you.'

He smiled down at her. 'I hope that when you feel you can tell me, you will.'

'Never,' said Beatrice, and, at that moment at least, meant it. 'I should get back, I'm making beds...'

But he made no movement at all to stand aside, and short of turning tail and going back the way she had come, there was no way of getting past him. She took refuge in polite conversation. 'Have you come down for a few days' rest?' she asked politely.

'No, I must go straight back. Ethel has a row of patients lined up for me to see this afternoon.'

'Oh—then why...?' She stopped before she said something silly.

'Did I come?' he finished for her. 'To see you, but now I find that this is not the right moment, after all.'

'What about?'

He laughed down at her. 'Getting married, Beatrice.'

The pretty colour in her cheeks paled. 'Oh, yes, of course. I—I hope that you will ask us all to your wedding.'

'You may depend upon that. Does Colin still write to you?'

The question took her by surprise. 'Yes, but I don't read his letters.'

'He's still in England?'

'I don't know. I've never looked at the postmark.'

'You really have forgotten him, haven't you?'

She said quietly, 'Oh, yes.' She smiled up at him, learning his face by heart.

'Heartwhole and fancy free,' he announced softly. 'Do you wonder what is around the next corner?'

She shook her head, held out her hand and said in a pleasant, polite and wooden voice, 'Goodbye, Oliver. We'll see each other again, of course, but it won't be—won't be the same.'

He took her hand. 'No, it won't.' He laughed down at her surprised face. 'Off you go and make your beds.' He touched her cheek lightly with a finger, and she turned and ran past him, furious with herself for crying. Thank goodness he hadn't seen that!

She raced upstairs and went on with the beds, and by the time she had finished she looked almost the same as usual. Only Ella, in the kitchen making the coffee, took a look at her pink eyelids and opened her mouth to speak, and then shut it again at her mother's frowning look.

It was three days later, when her mother had gone on her duty visit to Great-Aunt Sybil, Mrs Perry had gone home and Ella was at school, that Beatrice found herself alone in the house. Her father had gone to an outlying farm and Mr Sharpe had gone to the calf sale in Tisbury. It was another summer day, and she had opened all the windows and left the door to the kitchen open while she pottered to and fro, pulling radishes and cutting lettuce ready for supper that evening. Knotty was lying across the step, half asleep, and she had turned the radio on. Presently, she decided she would make a cup of tea and spend an hour in the garden before seeing to the few animals in the clinic.

She had her back to the door when Knotty suddenly got up in a flurry, barking madly, and when she turned round Colin was standing just inside the kitchen.

He was smiling, but she didn't much care for that; she waited silently for him to speak, feeling nothing but indignation at the way he had walked into the house in such a fashion. It made her feel better to see that he was disconcerted by her calm response to his appearance, but he recovered himself quickly.

'Took you by surprise, didn't I? I told you in my letters that I'd be back—perhaps you didn't believe me.'

'I don't read your letters. Will you go away, Colin? I'm busy.'

He grinned. 'I know where everyone is,' he told her, 'and you're here on your own for at least another hour. Time enough for us to have a little talk.'

'We have nothing to talk about.' She was suddenly furious. 'Get out, Colin. Why do you keep pestering me?'

'Because I have a very shrewd suspicion that

you're not going to marry that doctor of yours. It was a put-up job, wasn't it? Oh, I know all about it; you went to Europe with him, didn't you? I suppose you thought I'd be fool enough to go away. I don't give in so easily, Beatrice, my darling. He's not going to marry you, is he? For all I know he's already got a wife, so here you are, jilted. And don't deny it, there's not been a word about a wedding for weeks; I've had my ear to the ground in the village and I don't miss much. So now you should be glad that I still want to marry you. Of course, I shall expect a partnership—the practice is big enough to take a third man—a good salary in order to keep my wife in the comfort to which she has been accustomed and a decent house to live in.'

Beatrice said steadily, 'I think you're absurd. Perhaps I was infatuated with you for a few weeks, but now I really have no wish to see you again, so you can take no for a final answer and go away.' She added in a reproving voice, 'The weeks you have wasted, Colin!'

'Not wasted, my dear.' He had come into the kitchen and closed the door on a protesting Knotty. 'You can't deny any of the things I've said, can you?' He eyed her thoughtfully. 'I shouldn't be surprised to find that you're in love with this high and mighty doctor.'

He was astute. She had kept her face calm, but the look in her eyes gave her away, and he gave a triumphant chuckle. 'I thought so. All the more reason for you to reconsider marrying me. It would be one in the eye for him, wouldn't it? You must be feeling humiliated.' He clicked his fingers. 'Of course—he doesn't know! I shall enjoy telling him.'

'You're despicable, and he won't believe you.'

He had moved nearer and she had moved behind the kitchen table, facing him and taking comfort from its stoutness.

'Don't you believe it, darling. Can you imagine his tolerant amusement at your naïve idea? Just because he was good enough to help you out of a situation you didn't like, you have got besotted with him.'

'You are imagining a lot of nonsense,' Beatrice spoke with her usual calm, although her insides were shaking. She wasn't surprised when he said, 'I promise I won't tell, if you agree to marry me.'

She glanced at the old-fashioned clock behind him on the wall. In another half-hour or so her father would be back, and her mother too. She badly needed someone on her side, even Knotty, barking his head off again.

Knotty was barking at Ella, home earlier than usual from school and standing just out of sight, looking into the kitchen. Her first thought was to rush inside and help Beatrice bundle Colin out of the house, but prudence prevailed. Another man should deal with the situation. Mr Sharpe was just outside in the lane, talking to the vicar. She turned and ran round to the front of the house, just as the Rolls slid her handsome nose round the curve of the drive.

Ella didn't call out, she was too near the kitchen for that. She flew at the car, and the doctor slid to a halt, stopping with an inch or so to spare. 'Don't do that again, Ella, I very nearly died of fright.'

'Sorry, Oliver, do come! Thank heaven you're here. Colin's in the kitchen with Beatrice...'

He was a very big man and heavily built, but he reached the kitchen, opened the door and was inside while Ella was catching her breath. He hadn't appeared to hurry, yet there he was, leaning calmly against the doorjamb. Beatrice restrained an impulse to hurl herself into his arms, and wondered with a flash of temper at his almost casual attitude. True, he had come into the kitchen very fast. She gave him a rather tremulous smile, and thought thankfully that everything would be all right now.

Nobody spoke; the doctor gave the impression that he was half asleep anyway, and Colin was marshalling his wits, and Ella, who had slipped into the kitchen, held her tongue, which for her was unusual.

Presently Colin spoke. 'I'm staying in the village; it seemed a good chance to come and see Beatrice. I wanted to make quite sure that she was still open to persuasion to marry me. She might just as well— did you know, by the way, that the poor girl is head over heels in love with you?'

'Yes. I knew.' The doctor took a step, gripped

Colin by the arm and marched him outside, closing the door quietly as he went and Ella let out a gasp.

'Oh, do you suppose he's going to kill him?'

Beatrice was shaking like a jelly, furiously angry and so humiliated that she would cheerfully have sunk through the floor if that had been possible.

'I hope they kill each other,' she said with a snap.

Several minutes elapsed before the doctor returned. 'Did you knock him out?' asked Ella eagerly.

'Er—no. But I don't think he will be coming here again.' He hadn't looked at Beatrice. 'Do you suppose your mother would invite me to tea if you went and asked her? We'll be along presently.'

Beatrice made for the door, but she had to go round the table and Ella was ahead of her; besides, Oliver put out a leisurely arm and caught her hand as she tried to pass him.

He shut the door into the back hall as Ella went out, and stood leaning against it. 'Colin won't bother you again,' he said gently. 'I give you my word on that. Forget him, Beatrice.' He patted her shoulder in an avuncular manner. 'How very fortunate that Ella came home early from school, but I hope someone will warn her not to run full tilt into cars. I missed her by a couple of inches.' He gave her a kindly, impersonal smile. 'Shall we have tea? All this excitement makes one thirsty.'

She went ahead of him. He wasn't going to say anything about Colin's spiteful disclosure, and she was most grateful for that; she got red again just thinking about it. More than ever now she must avoid him. As they went into the drawing-room, her un-happy mind was already exploring the possibility of going to stay with one or other of the more distant family.

Ella must have said something, but no one men-tioned Colin as they had their tea. Oliver carried on an effortless conversation with her mother and father, completely at his ease, gave Ella a few useful hints about the biology paper she was preparing for her class, and without appearing to do so, drew Beatrice into the talk. He stayed some time then finally made his unhurried departure. From Beatrice's point of view, he couldn't go fast enough. She never wanted to see him again, although how she would be able to live without doing so was a moot point. She sum-moned up a stiff smile as he went, but she didn't go out to the car with the others. Instead she made some excuse about feeding Knotty. When they got back, she was so bracing in her manner that no one uttered a word about the afternoon's unfortunate event, and when she said in a bright voice that she fancied she would like a visit to an aged aunt of her mother's who lived with a great many cats in a cottage in Polperro, she met with an enthusiastic response.

'Why not, dear?' said her mother. 'There's that student coming from the veterinary college at Bristol; he can take over from you, and Aunt Polly will love to hear all the news.'

Which would have to be shouted, reflected
Beatrice, for the old lady was deaf.

But any port in a storm… To get away as soon as
possible was her one wish. She sat down that evening
and wrote to Aunt Polly, and then waited anxiously
for two days, during which no one mentioned either
Colin or Oliver to her. And when the reply came,
written in a spidery hand and violet ink, she showed
it to her mother.

'Aunt Polly wants me to go as soon as possible.
Tomorrow? The student comes the day after. I could
wait another day…'

'No, love, you go.' Her mother was slicing beans
and didn't look up. 'I'm sorry, darling. We all feel
for you, you know, even if we haven't said anything.'

Beatrice put the letter tidily back in its envelope,
taking time over it. 'Yes, Mother, and thank you all
for not saying a word. I don't think I could bear that.'

'A week or so away, darling, and you'll feel able
to cope again.'

'Yes, Mother, and please don't tell anyone where
I am.'

Mrs Browning, rightly deducing that anyone was
another way of saying Oliver, agreed.

Carol, with a few days off from her office, offered
to drive her down, and they left on a wet day which,
as they neared Cornwall, became shrouded in mist
as well. Between Tavistock and Liskeard it formed
a white wall which lasted until they neared the coast,
and as they took the road from Looe to Polperro the

mist lifted so that they had a glimpse of the little
town below, snug between high cliffs, the cottages
grouped around the small harbour. There were
houses on the hillsides on either side, too, and any
number of charming cottages tucked away on either
side of the one narrow main road. Aunt Polly lived
close to the harbour, up a tiny lane, with a steep flight
of steps leading to her front door. Carol parked the
car on the road and they went in together, already
seen by their aunt, who flung open the door and, in
the loud voice of the deaf, bade them welcome. Several cats came to welcome them too, and it took a
few minutes for greetings to be exchanged before
they all went indoors.

Aunt Polly was small and thin, with a ramrod-
straight back and a fierce-looking expression. No one
knew quite how old she was, and no one had dared
to ask, but it was thought that she was eighty at least,
although she didn't look much more than sixty. She
had refused help on several occasions, and if the family ventured to do more than write occasionally and
enquire as to her health she became remarkably testy.

She seemed glad to see Beatrice, partly because
Beatrice had a fondness for small animals and partly
because she didn't chatter, but she made no demur
when, after a late lunch, Carol said she must go back
home. Carol, she confided to Beatrice later, was a
nice girl, pretty too, but far too smart and fashionable.

'She's very clever,' pointed out Beatrice, on her

knees in the small sitting-room, brushing one of the cats. 'And everyone likes her.'

Aunt Polly snorted in a ladylike way. 'That's as may be. Why aren't you married? You must be all of seven and twenty.'

'I'm twenty-six, Aunt Polly.'

'Don't tell me you haven't had an offer?'

'Two serious ones.'

'And the others?'

'Not serious.'

'There's someone, I'll be bound, a pretty girl like you. He's married, I suppose?'

'No. Just engaged, and he's a friend, that's all.'

'A good basis for marriage, friendship. No good loving someone if you don't like them.' She removed a very large, fat tabby cat from her lap. 'We'll have tea. Go for a walk if you like before supper. I have it at eight o'clock. I like to go to bed early.'

The rain had stopped and the mist had lifted. The little town was quiet, the day tourists had left and most of the summer visitors had gone back home. Beatrice walked briskly round the harbour and climbed the cliff path on the other side. Tomorrow, she decided, she would walk to Talland Bay, unless Aunt Polly wanted her to do something else.

Aunt Polly suggested it over supper. 'I live in a nice little rut,' she explained. 'Don't think you have to entertain me. You can shop for me after breakfast and help me with the cats, and then go off and enjoy yourself until teatime.'

So Beatrice spent her days walking, taking sand-wiches and sitting on the cliffs to eat them, watching the sea and occasionally getting wet from the sudden rain showers. There was colour in her cheeks again, and she was even able to laugh a little over Colin's visit. She did her best not to think about Oliver, but when she did she got red in the face with shame, even though there was no one to see her. All the same, with two days of her holiday left, she felt that she could face everyone again. Given time, every-thing faded, even love, she supposed.

On the day before Carol was coming to fetch her, she took a last walk over the cliffs and then a stroll through the narrow, cobbled streets. It was the kind of morning which gave a hint of the autumn to fol-low, with a cool breeze which blew her plait over her shoulder and left her a little chilly although the sun was bright, hidden from time to time by great billowing clouds crowding in from the west. She stopped to look at a collection of pottery in one of the small shops; there were shelves of Cornish pis-kies, handmade and all different. One each for her sisters and another for her mother. There was a nice little painting, too, which would do for her father.

'Hello,' said Oliver gently.

She spun round and he caught her arm to steady her. The colour had left her face, now it came rushing back. 'How did you get here? Who told you?'

'I drove down and Mrs Perry told me...'

'But I asked Mother...'

'She said that she had promised not to tell—er—anyone. Mrs Perry happened to be there,' he added blandly.

'I'd rather not talk to you.' She was breathless, and any moment now she would burst into tears. 'I'm staying here with an aunt.'

'Yes, I know. A charming old lady. She's invited me to lunch.'

He took her arm and began to walk her away from the shops, back to Aunt Polly's house. 'A delightful place,' he observed chattily. 'Especially when the season is over. We must come again.'

'No,' said Beatrice, so loudly that several people looked at her.

The doctor came to a halt and turned her round to face him. 'You really are a goose,' he said, and smiled. Then, to the delighted interest of those passing by, he kissed her.

Beatrice closed her eyes and opened them again. He was still there, and she could feel his arms most reassuringly wrapped around her. 'You can't...' she began.

'Oh, but I can, and I will.' He kissed her again. 'The rest must wait.'

Beatrice sat through lunch in a bemused state, answering when spoken to, but taking no part in the conversation which Aunt Polly dominated with observations and tales about cats, and hers in particular.

'Beauty will have kittens in a few weeks.' She pointed to a grey Persian on the windowsill. 'She's pure bred, you know, thrown out when the people who owned her moved away.'

'Perhaps you will save one of the kittens for us,' suggested the doctor suavely.

Aunt Polly skewered his eyes with her own shrewd ones. 'Yes. Us?' She gave a chuckle. 'You shall have one for a wedding present.' She looked at Beatrice. 'You hear that, Beatrice?'

Beatrice muttered 'Yes, Aunt,' and didn't look up from the semolina shape she was pushing around her plate. She looked up pretty smartly when Oliver remarked that he would like to leave within the next hour. 'I'll wash up while you pack, Beatrice.'

'But I'm not…that is, Carol's coming for me tomorrow morning.'

'She was delighted when I suggested that I should take her place—there is some flower show or other that she wanted to go to.'

'So go and pack, child,' said Aunt Polly. 'I've enjoyed having you, but visitors do unsettle the cats, you know.'

So Beatrice packed and changed and got into the pink outfit, and presently went downstairs and found Oliver waiting for her in the hall. He took her bag from her and waited while she said goodbye and made her little thank-you speech, then he bent and kissed the old lady's cheek. 'You must come to the wedding,' he told her. 'I'll send a car for you.'

'The cats—they can't be left.'

'I'll find someone to mind them.' And Aunt Polly, by no means meek, nodded meekly.

The car was parked in a private car park half-way up the main street.

'No one is ever allowed to park here,' said Beatrice.

'I know.' He unlocked the car door and ushered her into the front seat, and went away to the man standing in a corner, presumably guarding his property. She could hear him laugh at something Oliver said, and watched money change hands.

She had been racking her brains for a suitable topic of conversation, something impersonal—the weather, the scenery, the state of the roads? A waste of time, for Oliver got into the car without a word, and beyond the remark that they would get back in time for tea he didn't speak. She found his silence disconcerting, and it lasted for the whole of the journey.

They were expected. Mrs Browning had tea ready and, since Carol was back from the show and Ella was there from school, there was no lack of conversation. And, if anyone noticed how quiet she was, no one said so.

Oliver got up to go after tea. 'You're staying down here?' asked Mrs Browning.

'Yes, possibly for a few days. It rather depends.'

He shook hands all round, but when he came to Beatrice he kissed her soundly without saying a word. When he had gone she stood in the hall for so long that her mother came back to look for her.

'Oh, Mother, I'm in such a muddle—he's not said a word...'

'He kissed you very thoroughly, love,' her mother pointed out.

Beatrice burst into tears. 'That's what I mean,' she cried.

She had thought that she would stay awake all night, but she slept at once and didn't wake until early morning. A lovely morning, too. It was going to be a splendid day. She got up and put on a skirt and top, and tied her hair back and slipped downstairs to let Knotty out and begin the climb up the hill. Perhaps she would be able to think clearly if she sat quietly and watched the sun rise in the pale sky.

She was almost at the top when she looked up. Oliver was there, watching her. She went on more slowly until she reached him, and he put out an arm and drew her close.

'Oliver, how did you know that I would come?'

'It's the best time of day. Do you remember, my darling, when we met? I fell in love with you then, and I believe you felt as I did, although you didn't know it then. You didn't know it for a long time, did you? I had to wait while you got Colin out of your system, so I allowed you to think that I was going to marry...'

'But why? There was no need.'

He kissed her slowly. 'I had to be sure, and I had to wait until you discovered that you loved me.'

'Oh, I do, I do. If you ask me, I'll marry you, Oliver.'

'I promised myself when we met that one day I would ask you to marry me on this very spot, and now I'm fulfilling that promise. Will you marry me, my darling?'

'Yes, I will. Darling Oliver, I think I'm going to cry.'

Her dark eyes had filled with tears, and he wiped them away with a finger, then kissed her very gently, pulled her down on to the fallen tree-trunk, and put an arm round her.

'A day for making a wish,' said Beatrice dreamily. 'Only I've got all I ever wished for, haven't I?'

'If you haven't, my dearest love, I'll make sure that you do.'

She kissed him for that.

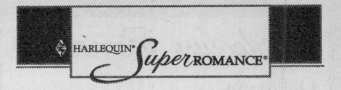

HARLEQUIN Presents

**The world's bestselling romance series...
The series that brings you your favorite authors,
month after month:**

Helen Bianchin...Emma Darcy
Lynne Graham...Penny Jordan
Miranda Lee...Sandra Marton
Anne Mather...Carole Mortimer
Susan Napier...Michelle Reid

and many more uniquely talented authors!

Wealthy, powerful, gorgeous men...
Women who have feelings just like your own...
The stories you love, set in exotic, glamorous locations...

HARLEQUIN Presents

Seduction and passion guaranteed!

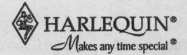

Harlequin® Historical

From rugged lawmen and valiant knights to defiant heiresses and spirited frontierswomen, Harlequin Historicals will capture your imagination with their dramatic scope, passion and adventure.

Harlequin Historicals . . . they're too good to miss!